His Unexpected Mail-Order Bride

Historical Sapphire Springs Book 1

Angie Campbell

Copyright 2018 by Angela Campbell

This is a work of fiction. Any resemblance
to persons, living or dead, or events
is merely coincidence.
Any unauthorized distribution of this work
or its characters is not permitted.

Cover by:
Erin Dameron-Hill
Award-Winning Cover Artist
www.edhgraphics.blogspot.com

Other Books in Reading Order:

Summer Obsession
Oh, Baby!
The Rodeo Star's Return

Available on Amazon.com

Prologue
Monday, February 27, 1871

Tobias Townsend looked up and frowned at the clouds slowly making their way across the morning sky. Thankfully, the snow had held off long enough, the funeral was over. Now, as he stood there, watching the undertaker's men start to fill the open grave, covering the coffin, the snow had finally started to fall. Not hard, yet. It was really no more than a little flurrying, but those clouds were threatening a whole lot more. He prayed for their sakes, they managed to get their job done before it really got started and made it difficult for them to get home. Snow this late in the month wasn't unheard of, but it wasn't the norm, either.

He crammed his hands in his pockets and turned away from the fresh grave of his new bride, wondering what had went so terribly wrong. He hadn't been in love with her. It had been more of an arranged marriage, than anything else, but he sure hadn't wanted her to die. She had suffered a broken neck when she had been thrown from a horse. A horse that was far too large for her to have been riding, in the first place.

Thinking back, he guessed he should have let her have the annulment. He hadn't realized at the time, just how badly she had wanted it. He had figured it was just nerves from being a new bride. He had told her they could take things slow and get to know each other first. Obviously, that hadn't been reassuring enough for her.

Truthfully, he hadn't been given the chance to rethink his decision on the matter. They hadn't been married even twenty-four hours when she took his horse and tried to run away. She hadn't made it two miles from the house, when she was thrown. An unusual winter storm had blown up that night. The horse had most probably been startled by a crack of lightening, and she hadn't known how to handle him, or been strong enough to control him. They had found a burnt tree, one of its larger branches lying on the ground, not fifty yards from where she had been found. After his horse came back to the house without her, they went looking for her. They found her lying in a puddle, where she had fallen. The dress she had worn for the wedding was now caked in red clay mud, her sightless eyes staring up at the darkening sky, and she was white as a ghost, like the blood had been entirely drained from her body.

He had still been trying to saddle his brother's mount, when his stallion came running back up to the barn. He knew immediately what he would find but had found himself still praying she was okay. He had even made the decision to give her whatever she wanted, if he found her alive. There was no way, if she was that desperate to get away from him, he wasn't going to let her go.

He made his way slowly back to the buggy, where Cade sat, silently waiting on him. He had stayed behind with Tobias to wait for all the other mourners to leave, while the rest of their brothers had gone back to the house with Mrs. Harris. She had told him, she would take the others, and go on ahead and get everything ready for the guests that were bound to show up now that the funeral was over.

All the neighbors in town had been bringing food by since early this morning. There were more casseroles and stews than he could count, along with a few pies and cakes. And that had been before he had left the house that morning. There was no telling how much food had been brought by since then.

He couldn't honestly tell you if he could eat right now, or not. His stomach was just too tied in knots. Probably more from his anger at her father, than from any grief over her death.

Her father had known she wasn't ready to get married. Instead of explaining that when he asked for her hand, the man agreed. Then apparently, forced her to go through with the marriage. If he had bothered to explain the situation, he and Rachel could have courted. Maybe she would have grown fond of him enough over time, she would have been willing to marry him after a few months. There had been no reason to rush to the altar if she wasn't ready.

Now, in less than three days after their wedding, she was dead and buried in the cold ground. It had been a tragic loss of a young life that could have been avoided if her father had only been willing to communicate. He shook his head in confusion, truly not understanding why her father hadn't just asked him to take the time to get to know her first.

He would have seriously consider beating some sense into the old man, if it wasn't for the fact he hadn't been seen since Cade had went to his house to tell him his daughter was dead. All Cade was able to tell him was, he hadn't seemed all that surprised when he told him what happened. He said he mumbled something under his breath, he didn't figure he was supposed to have heard, about her not being ready to marry, and now he had lost his only means. Whatever that had meant. He didn't believe Cade had heard everything. He alluded to the idea he thought the old man had been after money, and that was why he had forced her to marry him. Now, his cash cow was gone. He didn't figure they would ever see the old man again.

He climbed up beside Cade in the buggy and sighed, wondering if it was really worth the trouble to try and get married. He had never been around many women. Just his mother when she was still living. Some of the ranch hands had wives, and of course, there was the married women in town who helped their husbands run the various businesses. His problem was more, he didn't know how to interact with the younger, eligible women. He was always too busy running the ranch to even try to get to know anyone well enough to see if they would be a good fit for marriage. He just shook his head in frustration, just wanting to think about anything else, right at the moment.

"Are you going to be alright?" his brother asked, sounding concerned, but not bothering to look over at him. Tobias just appreciated the fact he hadn't gotten around to telling him, 'I told you so' yet. He figured he'd get around to it soon enough.

Cade had warned him he shouldn't marry Rachel, and he had stubbornly refused to listen. And no matter how much you wish things had been different, or that you had made different choices, you can't change the past.

"Yeah," he sighed, letting out a slow breath. "Let's just go home."

******

Tobias shook hands with the last of the mourners as they made their way out the door. It felt like it had been hours since he had started wondering when they were all going to start leaving. The entire town had been there, or at least it had felt like it. While he was grateful for their support, he was glad to see them go.

He was exhausted, both physically and mentally. He hadn't felt this level of exhaustion since his father and sister had died. All he wanted at the moment, was some time to himself. He turned from the front door, and slowly made his way toward the hallway.

"Hey, Tobias, where are you going?" Cade asked, turning to follow him.

"I just need to lay down for a while."

His younger brother frowned, trying to stop him with a hand on his arm. "Don't you need to eat supper?"

"Are you kidding? All we've done all afternoon, is eat. I don't think I'll need to eat for a week."

Cade gave him a concerned frown as he watched him turn toward the hall once again. He knew Tobias hadn't been in love with Rachel, but it seemed like he was taking her death extremely hard. He had barely said two words all day, and he wasn't sure he needed to be left alone, right now. "Are you sure you don't want to join the rest of us? I know you didn't eat as much as you are alluding to. You did more picking at your food, than eating it. Mrs. Harris made one of her famous apple pies," he said, hoping that would tempt him back the other way.

He nodded his head, then shook it, making it appear like he wasn't really sure what he needed right then. "Yeah, I'm sure. I just need to be by myself for a little while."

Cade sighed in defeat and watched as his older brother made his way down the hall with his shoulders slumped and disappeared into his room.

Tobias sat down on the bed, staring at the patch work quilt his mother had made for her and his father while she was still pregnant with his baby sister. She had been having trouble with the pregnancy almost from the time she had realized she was pregnant, and his father wouldn't let her do much more than sit and sew. He would only let her cook when she absolutely refused to be told no, and all the house cleaning had been left to his younger brothers.

It took him several seconds to realize he was staring at a piece of folded paper lying in the middle of the bed. It had blended in with the patchwork, and if he hadn't been staring at the quilt the way he was, he probably wouldn't have seen it at all. He reached over and pulled it towards him with two fingers, frowning in confusion. When he saw his name scrawled across it in a feminine handwriting, his frown deepened.

"Who would have been in here to leave me a note?" he mumbled out loud.

With a shake of his head, he picked it up to unfold. When he noticed the name at the bottom of the paper, his frown returned as he realized this was the first time he had been in here, for more than to change his clothes, since Rachel's death.

The note was short, and to the point. It simply said, 'Tobias, I'm sorry. I never wanted to marry you. Rachel'.

He jumped to his feet and had made it across the room and punched the solid oak door, cracking at least two of his knuckles, before he even knew what he was about. It was only a few seconds later when the door was flung open and he found himself facing his younger brother.

"What just happened? Are you alright?" Cade asked with concern.

Rather than answer, he just shook his head, and crumpled up the note to cram in his pocket, and silently made his way back to the bed, where he dropped on his face in defeat. He swore to himself then, he would never marry again.

Chapter 1
Tuesday, March 16, 1875

Tobias Townsend walked in through the backdoor of the two-story ranch house he occupied with his six brothers. Him being the oldest, he was more, or less the head of the household. The seven of them had inherited their father's ranch after a freak carriage accident had claimed the lives of both their father and baby sister Jolie, short for Jolene. She was barely three at the time. Their mother had died from childbirth when Jolie was born. Her whole name was Sarah Jolene, after their mother.

His parents had bought the land the ranch now sit on for little to nothing when they decided to move out west back in eighteen forty-seven. They had made it no farther than Missouri when their mother went into labor with him, and their father decided they had gone far enough. They were now hundreds of miles away from the painful memories and the homes they had grown up in, in Maine. At the time, his mother was barely seventeen, and his father only twenty-one.

They would have never been able to make the trip, much less purchase the land, if not for the inheritance his father had received after his own parents' death. All four of Tobias's grandparents had been stricken ill with fever, along with his mother's younger brother and sister, and passed away just weeks from each other. Thankfully his mother's older brother had already been married, and lived two states over, and had been untouched by the fever. Abraham Townsend, their father, had been an only child after his younger brother had died only days after his birth.

Tobias remembered his father saying once, he believed he and his mother had probably escaped just in time. He certainly believed, if they had stayed in Maine, they would have eventually died of the fever, as well. Instead, they had headed west, away from the pain and illness, and settled in what was now known as Sapphire Springs, Missouri. His father had been one of the four who had named the small town.

At the time, when his father had bought the nearly seven-hundred-acre ranch from the government, there wasn't but three other homes in the area, and they had to travel several miles to the nearest general store. His father, Abraham, along with David Harris, Joshua Miller and George Carter, was one of the original founders of the small town named for the incredibly clear, cold river that lay just to the east of where the Townsend ranch now sit.

The town, though small, now boasted of a general store, owned and operated by David Harris, along with a butcher shop, owned and operated by Joshua Miller. For the last twenty years George Carter had been the sheriff. The Townsend ranch had been large enough by the time the little town had really taken off, Abraham Townsend hadn't had the time to do anything but ranch. A lot of the town's growth had been attributed to the Townsend ranch.

Due to the size of the ranch, Tobias's father had to hire several ranch hands. Those ranch hands had brought their families with them. Due to the influx of people, a large number of them young couples with small children, they had to come up with a better way to get daily supplies. The town also now had a post office with a telegraph, a hotel and restaurant, tailor and seamstress, and a barber shop that sat next to the Sapphire Springs Saloon. Of course, there was also the sheriff's office with the livery stable next door, also ran by the Carter family. There was a stagecoach office, operated by Amos Ross. Then there was the school for the children, and a church with a small cemetery beside it that was maintained by the preacher, who's little house sat behind the church. No town would be complete, of course, without an undertaker and a hospital, which ironically, *or not*, sat side by side, to the west and just a little ways out of town.

The Townsend ranch house was known for being the only one in the area to have indoor running water and a flushing toilet. *Newly* built. Cade had seen a washroom like it in a hotel, in New York the year before and decided they just had to have one put in their house. Tobias still hadn't figured out Cade's justification for the expense, but since he had footed the bill all on his own, he could find no real reason to argue with him.

Tobias walked over to the kitchen counter and grabbed a glass and started pumping water from the pump. Once his glass was full, and the pump off, he turned to prop his tall, muscular body against the counter. He was just taking his first drink, when his younger brother Thaddeus walked in the kitchen.

"Hey, Tobias, I need to talk to you about something," he said, his voice shaking.

He looked at his younger brother, noting how much he had grown in the last few months. He was thinking they were going to need to take him to the tailor for some new clothes. They probably could buy him a few ready-made things, as well. He probably needed to check on Wally's wardrobe, while he was at it.

He raised an eyebrow at the blonde-haired boy, the spitting image of their late father, except for his coloring. "Why do you sound nervous? What do you need to talk to me about?"

The younger boy dipped his head, staring at the floor, and his shuffling feet. "You need to go into town and meet the stagecoach."

He laughed, shaking his own dark head. "Why would I need to meet the stagecoach?"

"Well...," the boy hesitated, gulping air. "You need to go get your mail-order bride," Thaddeus said in a rush, trying to get it out fast, before he vomited in the floor because of his nerves.

He stood up straighter, placing his water glass on the kitchen counter. "What do you mean, I need to go get my mail-order bride?" he asked on a laugh, thinking his brother was trying to make some really, bizarre joke. "I didn't order a bride."

"I know. I ordered her for you," he said, sweating, trying not to panic and run.

"What?" Tobias asked, thinking he may have fallen down the rabbit hole and was just now realizing it. He felt for sure he hadn't heard his younger brother right.

"I ordered her for you." He only managed to finish his answer because his brother was in such a state of shock, he had stood there in silence. "Her name is Sadie Johnson. She's coming from New York. She's supposed to arrive at one by..."

"Why?" Tobias barked, taking a menacing step toward his little brother. If it had been one of the older ones, he would have already had them laid out cold on the floor.

Thaddeus looked up with surprise in his eyes. "Why what?"

"Why did you send for me a mail-order bride?" he roared loud enough to nearly rattle the rafters.

Thaddeus stood up straighter, placing his hands on his hips. "You've scared off all the young women around your age in the area. Ever since..."

"Why do you think I need a bride?" Tobias snarled, working really hard to resist the temptation to grab his brother around the throat, and shake him.

"You need a wife. We need someone around here who can actually cook. Who will clean house during the day, while we're out on the ranch," he said, getting excited when Tobias didn't stop him again. Taking his silence as agreement, not realizing Tobias had been momentarily stunned again, he continued on. "She's supposed to even be able to keep the books straight. You know how much we all hate that chore."

Tobias snorted. "Somehow, I doubt she's going to be able to do that."

"There's only one way to find out," his little brother huffed.

He threw his hands up in the air with a roar. "I do not want a wife!"

"Why not?" Thaddeus asked, truly sounding confused.

"You know why."

His little brother stamped his feet, balling his hands on his hips. "We need a woman in this house."

"Then you marry her."

"She's expecting a twenty-seven-year-old man, not a sixteen-year-old kid," his younger brother said, throwing his own hands up in the air.

"Oh, now you call yourself a kid?" Tobias shouted, starting to pace the small kitchen like a caged tiger.

"You know what I mean. I'm not old enough to get married," Thaddeus shouted back.

During the course of their argument, both of them had steadily grown more agitated, and they had gotten quite loud. Their voices had risen enough in volume to draw the rest of the brothers to the kitchen with them. Though they had gone unnoticed, until Cade, raising his own voice above theirs, asked,

"What are you two shouting about?"

Tobias turned to face him, pointing back at Thaddeus, "This idiot sent for a mail-order bride for me. He thinks we need a woman in this house."

"Oh," Cade gasped, turning to look over at Thaddeus. "Is Miss Johnson due in today? I thought we had another week."

That wasn't anywhere close to the response he had thought he would get. "What?" Tobias snarled. "You mean you were a part of this?"

Cade just shrugged his wide shoulders, letting one of the others answer for him. "Well, not until a couple of weeks ago, when he told us what he had done," Ezekiel said, giving his brother a big grin.

"You too?" Tobias asked, this time just sounding shocked. "Have you three become a bunch of meddling, old women?"

"Now that really was uncalled for," Ezekiel chortled, obviously having way too much fun at his older brother's expense.

"Actually, we all know," Cade answered. "And we agree with him. I'll admit, at first I thought it was a bad idea, but after I gave it some thought, I reconsidered."

"Reconsidered?" their oldest brother roared. "Have you lost your mind? I don't want a wife, and you all know why."

"That's the biggest reason I think this is necessary," Cade said, spreading his feet and crossing his arms over his chest, like he was preparing for a fight. "I don't think you're going to let go of the past, until someone holds you down and forces a future on you."

"I won't do it. I don't care if you have all agreed, I'm not marrying this girl," he said with a shake of the head, walking back out the backdoor.

"Well, that went well," Cade grumbled in

irritation.

Ezekiel just chuckled. "I would say things went pretty good. The house is still standing."

******

Despite his assertion he would not marry her, Tobias's brothers had managed to browbeat him into meeting the girl at the stagecoach office. Cade had told him if he was going to send her back, then he was going to have to do it himself. If one of the others met her, they would bring her home with them, which would leave him still dealing with her when she got out to the ranch. They had all refused to leave her just standing there, wondering what had happened to him. They had made him give his word that he would go after her, and they knew he would never go back on his word, no matter how odious the chore he was set to do.

He had learned she really wasn't much more than a girl. Thaddeus told him she had just turned eighteen on January fifteenth when he gave him a description of her, so he could find her. He now stood in front of the post office, with his hands shoved in his pockets and a scowl on his face.

The post office was straight across the street from the stagecoach office. He was now staring at what had to be Miss Sadie Johnson talking to the town rogue, Michael Bayheart. Not that the town hadn't seen other rogues, but Bayheart was the only one who seemed to hang around after causing his brand of trouble.

Tobias started across the street, the scowl on his face growing darker with each step he took. He reached her side in time to hear the very pretty, little brunette introduce herself to Bayheart.

"I'm Sadie Johnson. I'm waiting for Tobias

Townsend," she said, taking a step back from the rogue, who for some reason, was doing everything short of wrapping his arms around her. Tobias was sure, if it wasn't for them standing on a very public street, he wouldn't have been restraining himself even that much.

"Well, speak of the devil. You are in luck. Here he is," Bayheart said, giving her a very predatory look. "Townsend," he said in greeting. "I was unaware you had any family other than your brothers."

"I don't," Tobias growled.

"Oh, I'm not related to him," she gasped, working to catch her breath. She was in a state of shock. He was absolutely the most gorgeous man she had ever laid eyes on. He had to be at least three inches over six feet, with the broadest shoulders she had ever seen on a man. His hair was dark and wavy, and cut short enough she wouldn't have noticed if he hadn't taken his hat off when Bayheart first introduced them. And his light blue eyes held a touch of sadness in them she hoped she could help heal. "Not yet, anyway. I'm here to marry him. I'm his mail-order bride."

"You've got to be kidding me," the man chuckled. "Townsend doesn't want to get married. Do you, Townsend?"

"If you don't mind, Bayheart, I need to get Miss Johnson settled into a room at the hotel for the night," Tobias snarled, taking first her bag, then her arm to turn her toward the hotel down the street. "Is this your only luggage?" She just nodded her head in answer, biting her bottom lip and glanced back at Bayheart.

"Miss Johnson," Bayheart called out behind them. "When he dumps you at the altar, come find me. I'll show you how a real man is supposed to treat a woman as beautiful as yourself."

Sadie glanced back at him again, a shocked look on her pretty face. When she turned back to Tobias, she had tears in her eyes. "What does he mean, you don't want to get married? Then why would you have sent for me?"

"Ignore him. He doesn't know what he is saying. He's just trying to stir up trouble. That seems to be the only thing he is good at," Tobias said, not looking up at her. He had to find a way to get her back on the stage tomorrow without the rogue finding out. He may not want to marry her, but he didn't want to see her life ruined by the likes of Bayheart.

"Then why are you taking me to the hotel?" she said, panting, struggling to keep up with his long stride.

He slowed down, matching his pace to hers when he realized how much she was struggling. "I figured you would want a night to rest, and I can't take you home with me until after the wedding," he said, opening the hotel door for her. "This way you can get a bath and be well rested in the morning when I come back to town for you. You really don't want to get married with all that dust from the stage covering you, do you? It was my thought that women liked to be fresh and all prettied up for these things."

She gave him a big grin. "Yes, I guess you are right. A bath sounds really nice."

Once she was settled in her room, and washed up a bit, she went back down to the lobby where he asked her to meet him. She walked over to where he stood propped against the counter, giving him a big smile. "Okay, what did you want to do now?"

He swallowed hard, staring at her like a man dying of thirst. It was amazing what getting rid of a little dirt and straightening her chestnut curls had done. He had known she was beautiful the moment his eyes had landed on her from across the street, but now, with her bright blue eyes shining with happiness and her delicate pale skin washed of the dust of the trail, she was absolutely stunning. She was a tiny little thing in comparison to his six feet three inches. The top of her head just reached his chin. If he were to marry her, he'd always be afraid he was going to break her.

"Mr. Townsend, are you okay?" she asked, her beautiful face puckering up, her delicate brows drawing down in concern.

He shook his head to clear it of his current thoughts. "Sorry. Are you hungry? You've been on the stagecoach for a few days. I'm sure you didn't get much to eat."

"Yes, something to eat sounds wonderful," she said, breathing a sigh of relief, thinking she had made the right choice, coming out here to marry him.

He gave her a big smile. "I thought you might feel that way. Does going over to the Sapphire Springs Café sound good to you?"

"I guess," she answered with a shy smile. "Obviously you would know better than I would."

"Well, how do you feel about fried chicken and mashed potatoes with gravy?" he asked with a grin. If he ever did wish to marry, he would hope to find someone like her. She truly was very beautiful. Unless she was doing an incredible acting job, she also had the sweetest nature a man could ever hope for.

"That sounds amazing."

"Good," he grinned. "Tuesday is fried chicken. Roast beef is Friday. My second favorite."

Originally, he had planned on just dropping her off at the hotel, then leaving. Now he felt it was necessary to give the impression he intended to marry her, without an outright lie. So, placing her hand in the crook of his elbow, he led her out the door and across the street to the restaurant.

She picked up the skirt of her dress, doing her best not to pick up anymore dust, and smiled at him. "Are you saying fried chicken is your favorite?"

"Yes, I love fried chicken, and cherry pie. Though apple is a definite close second."

"I'm starting to get the feeling you really love to eat," she laughed softly.

"Eating might just be my favorite pastime," he grinned. "I hope you are ready to cook."

She laughed softly, smiling up at him. He was going to have to get her out of Sapphire Springs fast, he thought to himself, when he realized what he had just said, or he was going to be in *deep* trouble. He feared he *already* was.

Chapter 2
Wednesday, March 17

Ezekiel made his way down the street toward the hotel after leaving Wally with the preacher's wife at the church, Cade, Zach, Josiah and Thaddeus with him. They were getting ready for their oldest brother's wedding. A wedding he didn't know he was going to have, yet. When they cooked up this scheme yesterday, while Tobias was in town meeting Sadie, they hadn't thought about today being Saint Patrick's Day. The entire town looked like it had been splattered with green oil paint, and the holiday probably accounted for the number of people already in town today. There had never been an official town celebration for the holiday, but there was a number of Irish descendants living in and around Sapphire Springs, and there was always a festive feeling on the day.

Their mother had been Irish and had loved the holiday. He could remember her still having quite an Irish brogue when he was little. He smiled at a little girl who ran by with green ribbons bouncing in her curly blonde hair, thinking his mother would approve of her oldest son getting married on Saint Patrick's Day. He just hoped his brother came around to agreeing soon.

The brothers passed several people on their way to the hotel, getting stopped several times for individuals to ask them if it were true their oldest brother was getting married today. If one person told them they were going to be there, fifty did. Most just wanting to see if he would really go through with it. What they didn't understand, was all of them attending the wedding was one way to make sure Tobias went through with it. That was why they had made sure to tell a couple of their friends to make sure and spread the word. By the time they made it inside the hotel, he was starting to think the whole town might just show up at the church, making their brother's wedding the biggest one in the history of the town.

Ezekiel walked up to the hotel counter with the four others behind him. "Do you think we have enough Irish in our heritage to make getting married on Saint Patrick's Day lucky?" he asked, looking around at all the green. Someone had hung a green banner around the room, wishing everyone a happy Saint Patty's Day, and there were green tablecloths on the tables in the small dining area for the hotel guests that chose to eat there instead of across the street at the café. Mostly the tables were used for breakfast, or afternoon tea with a little dessert. Mrs. Slater didn't offer a lot of variety. Just something for those who were too tired from traveling to want to get out and go across the street.

"Well, Mom was Irish, with the red hair and temper to prove it," Zach chuckled.

"You remember her temper?" Ezekiel asked, giving him a skeptical look.

"Well, I remember her getting really loud when I was in trouble," he replied sheepishly.

Cade chuckled, shaking his head at his two younger brothers. He remembered more about his mother's temper than her getting loud. He used to run and hide in the barn when he knew he or one of the others were going to be in trouble. Problem was, it never really worked. She always knew just where to look. Thinking back now, he realized he probably should have tried to come up with a different hiding spot, but he never thought to.

He slapped the other two on the back and declared. "I believe a little Irish goes a long way,"

"Let's hope so. I'm afraid we're going to need all the luck we can get," Josiah added.

Ezekiel shrugged, doing his best to think positive. "Don't worry. Everything's going to work out just fine. We're only trying to do what's best for him."

"I know we said that, but I didn't expect him to get so angry when he found out."

"Come on, Joe. We all knew starting out, he wasn't going to go down easy."

"Yeah, I know," he said, picking up a paper cutout of a four-leaf clover someone had painted green. "Do you think wishing on a paper four-leaf clover would work? Maybe we could fold it up and stick it in his pocket."

It was just now after eleven in the morning. They had all left the care of the ranch with the hired hands, and their oldest brother still asleep. They were all planning to ambush their pigheaded brother to make sure this wedding took place. Like Cade had said, they were going to have to force a future on him, or he would never get over the past.

Speaking of, Cade laid his big hand on the counter, leaning over only far enough to ding the little bell to alert someone of their presence. It wasn't but a couple of seconds before the owner's wife, Mrs. Annie Slater came out of the office door located behind the counter.

"Well, hello boys. I hope you're having a good Saint Patrick's Day."

"Hello to you, as well, Mrs. Slater." he said giving her a big smile. "And that remains to be seen. Is your husband around?"

"He sure is," she smiled back. "Are you all here to

fetch your brother's bride? Are you all afraid she's going to run off?"

"We are here to fetch her, but we hadn't thought of her running off," Cade said with a frown.

"She's more likely to with all five of you here to fetch her," she said, giving them all a concerned look. "You are a little likely to scare her. You all look rather intimidating, being as big as the lot of you are. She might think you look like you are marching her off to prison. She is a little thing, and she is probably nervous already. That can make the imagination rather active."

"Oh, no. Zach and I are here to wait for Tobias," Cade grinned, shaking his head. "We're going to escort him to the church. Just in case he develops cold feet."

She gave him a curious look, crossing her arms in front of her. "You're not afraid he'll grow cold feet before he gets here?"

"Oh, no. Some of the hired hands are going to make sure he gets here," he grinned.

She shook her head at him. "Why do I have this feeling in my gut that you all are up to something?"

Cade just gave her a big grin, full of confidence, not saying a thing. The lady was smart, *for sure*, but she didn't need him to tell her that.

Tobias would be here, because he didn't know yet that he would be getting married. He was also certain he would make it on time, because he had asked the man he had left in charge, John Wilson, to make sure and cause a loud disturbance to wake his brother up about thirty minutes after they all left. He told him, he didn't care what the disturbance was, just as long as his brother didn't realize it was intentional. Of course, he also added, make sure no one, or any of the animals got hurt. They didn't need anyone down with an injury, or to lose any of the animals over a little prank.

She noted his stubborn look, and just nodded her head in resignation. "Well, if they are here to fetch Miss Johnson, what do you need my husband for? She is in room two oh one. It is right at the top of the stairs. I know for a fact she is already dressed and packed to go. She had a bath taken up two hours ago. She is really excited to be marrying your ornery brother, today."

"Well, Ma'am, she's not met us, as of yet. Tobias did mention she had met your husband," Cade grinned. "We thought he might help ease things along by introducing these three to her. You know, to make it less *intimidating* for her. Like you said, they're liable to scare her running for sure, if they just show up at her door unannounced."

"Oh well, in that case," she grinned back, still feeling like they were up to something, but her gut also told her it was probably for the best. "I'm sure he'll be more than happy to help. I've not met the young lady yet, myself. I only saw her from the back, for a second on her way up the stairs yesterday. He said she was a real pretty young lady, and sweet as the day is long."

Cade gave her a curious frown. "You did say he was here, didn't you? Is he busy?"

"Oh, sorry," she said with a shake of her head. "He is here or will be momentarily. He just went to the post office to send off a letter. We have a young niece coming in to visit with our Dawn. Well, I say young. She's seventeen. Anyway, he should be getting back any second, now."

Just then, the man in question came around the end of the counter. "Hello, boys. In town for your brother's wedding? I don't think I've ever seen a wedding on Saint Patrick's Day before. The church is already filling up. I'm betting most of the town will be there," Mr. Slater chuckled. "I'm planning on being there myself. My guess is, most of the town want to see if he'll really go through with it. I know for one, Jeremiah Miller said he'd be willing to marry her if your brother backs out."

"Better him than that no account, Michael Bayheart," Mrs. Slater said with a sniff. "He was sniffing around her skirts when she first got off the stage. Your brother got to her just in time, before any tongues could start to wagging."

"Now, Annie, don't get started talking about that man," Mr. Slater huffed. "I've never seen him take advantage of the uninformed."

"He's ruined more than one reputation," she said, giving her husband a dirty look.

"Well, the young ladies in question knew beforehand he wasn't likely to marry them *when they threw themselves at him*. Apparently, he had already turned them both down, more than once. They also should have known their fathers weren't likely to confront him. The only ones around these parts faster with a gun, is Tobias, and the sheriff's son, Johnathan."

"Well, he should have been the one to leave town, not those girls and their families."

"Alright, Woman, that's enough," Mr. Slater snapped. "This is to be a happy day. No more ranting. Now, what can I do for you boys?" Mr. Slater asked, effectively dismissing his wife by turning his back on her and missing the dirty look on her face. Cade figured the older man would get an ear full later, even though he agreed with him where Michael Bayheart was concerned. The man never went after innocent women. Unless they did the chasing, he didn't interact with them at all. At least, not anymore. Before, he would only talk to them with a chaperon present. How anyone had ever believed that mess over those two girls, he would never understand.

Cade grimaced with a shake of his head. "We need you to introduce these three to Tobias's bride. They're going to escort her to the church. Zach and I are going to wait down here to make sure Tobias makes it to the church on time."

"Does Tobias know you planned all this?" Mr. Slater asked, giving Cade a huge grin.

"Well, no, as a matter-of-fact, he doesn't," Cade grinned back. "We want to make sure he doesn't chicken out. After his past experience, he's still a little nervous."

"That's to be expected," Mr. Slater said with a nod of his head, walking back around the counter. "Come on then. Follow me. I'll introduce you to the young lady."

Ezekiel, Josiah and Thaddeus followed after the older man, while Cade and Zach turned back toward the doors, to stand guard. The four came to an immediate halt when Mr. Slater reached the first door on the left and stopped to knock.

The door opened just a crack, and all they could see at first was one bright blue eye and a delicate, pale cheek.

"Yes?" a soft feminine voice asked.

"Miss Johnson, do you remember meeting me yesterday? I'm Mr. Slater. I own the hotel."

They heard her breathe a sigh of relief as the door came the rest of the way open to reveal a tiny woman, dressed in a white dress, trimmed with green ribbon. Well, she was tiny compared to the men standing before her. "Yes, of course. Sorry about that. I was expecting Mr. Townsend. When it was someone else, it made me nervous. I really hate traveling alone." She glanced past his shoulder with a curious look.

"Well, that's understandable for a young lady,

like yourself," he said, giving her a reassuring smile. "These young men here are some of your intended's younger brothers."

"*Some* of his younger brothers?" she asked, her eyebrows shooting up into her hairline.

"Yes, Ma'am," Thaddeus whispered, staring at the floor, a blush staining his cheeks. "We have three other brothers. Cade and Zach are down there, waiting for Tobias. Wally's already at the church with some of the ladies from town, getting it ready. We're here to escort you to the wedding."

She gave him a soft smile, reaching over to lay her hand on his shoulder. "I think that sounds like a wonderful idea. I really appreciate that. What's all your names?" she asked, looking over to the one who had to be the oldest of the three.

Ezekiel grinned at her and laid his own hand on Thaddeus's other shoulder. "The shy one here is Thad, short for Thaddeus. The big, quiet brute behind me is Josiah, but be warned, both Cade and Zach are bigger than he is. We sent them with Tobias in hopes of making you less nervous."

"You can call me Joe if you like, Ma'am. My brothers do," the young man in the back said, stepping forward to take her small hand in both of his larger ones. "Wow, you really are small."

Sadie gave a soft laugh. "Well, I never really thought so, myself. Please, call me Sadie. We'll all be family before the day is out."

"Yes, Ma'am... I mean, Sadie," he said, taking a step back.

She grinned, then looked back at the one she had yet learned the name of. "So, that leaves just you."

"What? I'm sorry," Ezekiel said, looking confused.

She gave another soft laugh. "Your name?"

"Oh, sorry. I'm Ezekiel," he answered, grinning

at her.

"So, why are you all escorting me?" she asked, starting to sound a little nervous. "I thought Tobias planned to come and get me himself."

"Well, he did plan to, but we stepped in," Ezekiel answered, giving her a concerned look.

"Oh. Why, do you not like me?" she asked, blushing crimson.

"We like you just fine, Sadie," he said, trying to use a reassuring tone.

Giving him a confused look, she asked, "Then why did you want to step in?"

"Well," Ezekiel said, giving her a big grin, "while this is not the typical set of circumstances for a wedding to take place, we wanted it to be as traditional as possible."

"Traditional?" she asked, still sounding confused.

"Yes, Ma'am. The groom must not see the bride before the wedding," Thad said, still staring at the floor.

"Oh," she smiled shyly. "I hadn't thought of that."

Noting how uncertain of herself she still sounded, Ezekiel gave her a reassuring smile. "We're all really happy our brother is marrying you."

"Oh," she said on a breath. "I was afraid maybe you were here to stop the wedding."

"No, Ma'am," Thaddeus said, finally looking up at her. "It's the best idea he's ever had, and you sure are pretty," he said, causing himself to blush. In spite of his obvious embarrassment, he managed to finish with, "We definitely want him to marry you."

"Thank you, so much. I'm really happy to hear that," she said, barely holding back the tears. She hadn't known what to expect when she got to Sapphire Springs. Seeing that her future husband's family was more than ready to accept her into the fold, filled her with a very strong emotion she couldn't quite name right then.

"You look really pretty in your wedding dress," Josiah added with a huge grin. "Did you use green ribbon because you hoped to get married on Saint Patty's Day?"

"Well, I thought I was going to be married as soon as I got here," she answered shyly. "I knew it would be somewhere around the holiday. I'm hoping, getting married today is a sign of good things to come."

He nodded his head in response. "I'm sure it will be."

Ezekiel cleared his throat to bring her attention back to him. "Speaking of making your wedding more traditional, Thad had something he wanted to ask you." He gave his little brother a gentle push forward, looking down to nod his head at the teenage boy.

Thaddeus gulped, turning red once again. "Miss Johnson, will you allow me to walk you down the aisle? With the absence of your father, you would be walking on your own, and that doesn't seem right to me. We all decided that I get to walk you down the aisle, if you'll let me."

"I think that would be a wonderful idea," she answered, nearly crying again. She had never gotten around to explaining to Tobias in her letters why she was willing to travel so far and be a mail-order bride. Even if he had told them what he did know of her, they would have no way of knowing her father had died two years ago. Her mother had urged her to find a suitable husband because they were quickly running out of funds to support themselves with. She wasn't sure how much longer her mother would be able to live on what she had left, but she knew it wasn't nearly long enough.

******

By the time Tobias reached the hotel that morning, it was already close to noon. He was worried he might miss the stagecoach that would take Sadie back to Saint Louis, where she could take a train back east. The stagecoach came into town once a week and left out the next day. Sapphire Springs was far enough off the beaten path, they were lucky they had a stagecoach come through even that often. If he missed today's coach, it would be another week before he had a chance to send her back home. That was something he couldn't allow to happen if he wanted to protect Sadie from the likes of Michael Bayheart.

He had arrived in town to the reminder that today was Saint Patrick's Day. Between the headache he had and all the green, he felt like he was seeing giant, floating shamrocks in the air. Any other time, he would be enjoying the holiday with everyone else, but right now, he was just sick of all the green. He shook his head, wondering why he felt a need to vomit. Maybe it wasn't the green at all, and he was just sick.

Due to his over sleeping, and the headache he woke up with, he was already in a foul mood by the time he reached the hotel lobby. Finding both Cade and Zach there, waiting on him, didn't help his disposition one bit.

"What are you two doing here?" he growled, giving them both a dirty look before trying to push past them.

"Saving you from yourself," Cade said, grabbing him under one arm as Zach did the same on the other side. Tobias wasn't a small man by anyone's standards. Still, at six feet three inches, he was a few inches shorter than both of his younger brothers. While Cade, at six and a half feet tall was probably done growing at twenty-five, Zach wouldn't even be twenty until October of this year. At six five already, there was no telling how tall he would get before he was done growing.

Needless to say, they had his feet dangling inches from the ground. Even if he thought he could get the better of them both at the same time, which he knew better than to even contemplate the idea, he had no way of breaking free in this position to even try.

They immediately turned back toward the door, Tobias hanging between them. They both nodded their heads at the Slaters, who stood behind the check-in counter. Mr. Slater just chuckled and shook his head at them. Mrs. Slater smiled and waved, wishing him good luck. They both seemed to be acting like this was a perfectly normal occurrence, and it was obvious he wasn't going to get any help from either one of them.

"You two idiots," he growled. "Put me down. I'm supposed to meet Miss Johnson."

"We know, but we're not letting you send her back east," Zach said, opening the door with his free hand so they could step outside.

"Why else do you think I spent an entire dinner, spiking your sweet tea with just a little bit of whiskey?" Cade chuckled.

"Yeah. Lucky for us, it doesn't take much whiskey to put you out all night, and make you sleep like the dead."

"I wondered why the tea was so sweet last night," he grumbled. "It tasted like you had used a whole year's worth of sugar in that stuff, and I felt like I was waking up from a yearlong nap."

"Yeah, I might have got a little enthusiastic toward the end of the night. Sorry about that," Cade said, not sounding at all contrite. "Once you started to get a little drunk, I wasn't as worried about you tasting the whiskey."

"That certainly would explain my headache and the floating shamrocks," he grumbled under his breath, but apparently not under enough.

"Floating shamrocks?" Cade chuckled, nearly losing his grip for a second. A second, Tobias failed to take advantage of, making his mood even more sour.

He snarled at his brother, choosing to ignore his comment on the floating shamrocks. "I don't see how this is going to work if I don't show up to escort her from the hotel," Tobias reasoned, grasping at straws. He knew his brothers well enough to know they had prepared ahead of time.

"Oh, don't worry," his aggravating brother grinned. "We have that covered. Ezekiel, Josiah and Thaddeus are here to escort her to the church."

"I had wondered why there wasn't anyone at the house when I woke up. I just figured as late in the day as it already was, you were all out working on the ranch. I foolishly thought there was no way you could attempt to force me to marry her. I should have known none of you would let this drop without more of a fight," he grumbled to himself, wondering how he let himself be fooled so easily.

"We have to hurry and get you to the church," Zach urged. "The others will be right behind us. Thaddeus was watching from upstairs to see when you showed up."

"That might not work. She's never met them," he tried again, mentally crossing his fingers. He struggled between them, trying to see if he could get at least one of them to lose their grip, but without any luck. They didn't even seem to notice as they made their way down the dusty boardwalk, toward the church. Not really surprising, since both of them had spent most of their lives wrestling with cattle and horses in one way or another. The type of work they all did for a living tended to make the body strong.

They got a few strange looks, and more than one person stopped to stare. He was even sure he heard more than one burst of laughter, but no one bothered to ask what was going on. He was starting to think the whole town had gone daft.

"Already taken care of," the two said together. "We all came in early to town, so they could meet her," Cade continued. "Old Man Slater introduced them to her. We remembered you saying she met him yesterday while you were checking her in at the hotel."

"The pastor might not have time for a wedding today. I noticed there was a big crowd at the church," he added, praying that crowd wasn't there for his wedding.

"Pastor Winters is waiting at the church for you," Cade said with a grin. "That crowd is there to see you and Miss Sadie get married. So, stop trying to wiggle your way out of this. Your goose is cooked."

"It's already Miss Sadie, to you?" he snarled, glaring at Cade.

"I'm practicing. I don't want to call her Mrs. Townsend after you two are married," he chuckled. "She'll be my sister-in-law after all."

He shook his head, feeling the panic rise up his throat. "Are you sure the preacher is at the church?" he asked out of desperation.

"Yeah, he's waiting with Wally, along with half the town," Zach said, barely stifling a laugh.

He gave them both a belligerent glare and huffed. "Don't think having half the town there will stop me from putting her back on that stagecoach."

"That's exactly what we think. No matter what, you would never embarrass an innocent young woman like that," Cade answered back.

"Besides, the stagecoach is already gone today," Ezekiel added. "It left early, because everyone who was schedule to leave out on it had already made it to the stagecoach office and were waiting to leave by eleven o'clock."

Tobias huffed, ignoring Ezekiel to address Cade. "I'm not the one to blame for her eventual embarrassment."

"Do you really think that's going to matter? The damage will still have been done."

"I'm going to strangle both of you for this."

"If you fight one of us, you're going to have to fight all of us. Even Wally," Cade stated with very forceful certainty.

In no time at all, they had made it all the way down Main Street to where the church sat. He could tell by all the noise coming out of the open doors, the church was already full to bursting. Unfortunately for him, his brothers were right. He would never embarrass Sadie by rejecting her in front of all these people. He had been through something of the sort himself a couple years earlier. Unless he found a way out of this situation soon, which didn't seem likely, he would be getting married within the hour.

When Tobias walked in through the doors at the back of the church, what he saw almost stopped him dead in his tracks. Between all the people and the green from the decorations that had obviously been moved to the church for his wedding, he was feeling even more like vomiting than before. "I didn't realize we knew this many people," he whispered to Cade.

"Well, apparently we do," Cade whispered back.

"Even if that's true," he grumbled, "I would think a wedding in the middle of the day would be a big inconvenience for over half of these people."

"It probably is. I think most of them are betting

you won't go through with it. They don't realize their being here is what will ensure you do go through with it."

"I didn't ask for a mail-order bride," he snarled. "You all know why I don't want to get married."

"Tobias, you have to let go of the past, at some point," Cade said with a shake of his head.

"No, I don't," he snarled back.

"Well, the rest of us are praying Miss Sadie can change your heart on the matter. This is probably your last chance at happiness."

"I am happy. With the way things are."

"No, you're not, and the rest of us aren't going to be able to move on with our own lives until we feel like you are more settled. I'd like to get married soon, myself. Heather will be twenty in another year and a half. Her father has already given me permission to marry her."

"I didn't realize you were planning on marrying so soon."

"Why else do you think I've been working on building my own house? I want to be on the ranch with you all, but I want to give her, her own house to run. Her own kitchen."

"I'll be bringing Sadie into the big house with all of the rest of you."

"Yes, but it'll be her house to run, and as the rest of us marry, we'll leave the big house. Of course, by the time Thad and Wally marry, hopefully you and Sadie will have a bunch of little ones of your own."

"No, no little ones," he said, shaking his head vigorously, almost sounding scared.

"Oh, I think you'll change your mind. I have a good feeling about all of this. I think you and Miss Sadie will have more children than the rest of us."

"You don't know what you're talking about."

"We'll see," Cade said, a grin on his handsome

face as he turned to walk away.

Tobias stood at the front of the church, his brow furrowed. His brother had given him something to think about. He hadn't realized how much they worried about him. It may not be his fondest wish to get married, but that was no reason for the rest of them not to.

Tobias turned to face the back of the church when he heard the big, double doors open, and his thoughts scattered. Sadie stepped through the doors, his younger brother, Thaddeus by her side. He was apparently standing in for her father and giving her away. He watched them slowly make their way up the aisle, mesmerized by how truly beautiful she was. He had noticed yesterday, but today with her all cleaned up and well rested and dressed in a dress that had obviously been made for their wedding, she was more breathtaking than he could have ever imagined. He wondered if he should take it as a sign that her dress was trimmed in green and they were getting married today, of all days.

Several minutes later, he stood in the yard between the church and the pastor's house. They had decided to have a picnic style reception, with all the ladies of the town pitching in with food and a cake with punch. They had been blessed with a warmer day, with only a soft breeze blowing. Quite unusual for this early in March. They had decided to take advantage of the unexpected, pleasant weather, and let everyone get some fresh air while they mingled.

He could barely remember the ceremony, only thinking it seemed to have been quick. Like the preacher had been told to make it short, to keep him from fleeing before it was over. His responses must have been the right ones. Everyone seemed happy. Well, everyone except for him, that is. He just didn't want to be responsible for someone else's misery in the future. One thing was for sure, he would never look at Saint Patrick's Day the same, ever again. Whether or not that turned out to be a blessing or not, remained to be seen.

Chapter 3
Wednesday, April 7

The happy glow Sadie felt at the wedding only lasted until they got out to the Townsend ranch, where Tobias unceremoniously dumped her without a word. Not even a goodbye, see you at supper. He had turned and stomped back to the door, slamming it on his way out. By the time the shock wore off enough for her to follow him, and she raced out to the porch, he and his horse were just a speck on the horizon.

When she had turned back to the others to ask what was wrong, they all just shook their heads with a mix of expressions on their faces. Some sad, some confounded. One or two, even angry. She had thought then, maybe they were angry with her. It hadn't taken long to realize it was none other than Tobias they were angry with.

They had all in turn, came over to her, and giving her a hug, apologized for their idiot brother. Their words, not hers. Even though, now she agreed with them. At the time, she was just hurt by his behavior. They had all repeatedly assured her everything would work out. She just had to have faith, and patience.

That had been three weeks ago, and nothing had changed. He had given her, her own room down the hall. It felt like he had intentionally given her the room farthest from his own. All his brother's rooms were upstairs, and there were three more rooms between theirs. That may not have been what he was thinking, but she had no way of knowing. He did his best to avoid her. He did so well in fact, she only saw him at mealtimes with his brothers. He made sure to come to the table after the rest of them were seated and was the first one up and gone. She never found a private minute to talk to him.

Each night after supper, he would leave the house almost at a run. He'd take off toward town so fast, you'd think the devil was on his heels. All she wanted was for him to give her a chance to prove she could be a good wife. He wouldn't even give her a chance to ask what it was she'd done so wrong. When he had kissed her at the wedding, she had felt like every dream she'd ever had was coming true. If someone would have asked her right then, she would have said he felt the same way.

Tonight, after he had left, she had looked to all his brothers for an answer. They had tried, whole heartedly, to reassure her she had done nothing wrong. They just kept telling her, Tobias had something he had to work out.

It had taken her several more minutes to wear one of them down enough to get him to tell her where Tobias ran off to every night. The rest of them had sat there with stern looks on their faces, shaking their heads. If she heard them tell her once she couldn't go, she heard it twenty times. While she got the feeling, they were all just concerned, they all seemed to think Tobias would be angry. Well, quite frankly, anger would be much more preferable than stone cold silence. At least it was an emotion almost guaranteed to get him talking.

So now, here she was, stomping down the center of main street, headed for the only saloon in the whole town. The dirty rascal. "So much for getting married on Saint Patrick's Day being a good sign of things to come," she grumbled to herself. His brother Thaddeus had told her she could find Tobias there.

She was getting sick of being ignored. She was starting to think he had married her just to do his laundry and cook for him. Now she finds out he's been spending his nights getting drunk. She didn't even know where he was sleeping it off at. It certainly wasn't at home with her. If she found out it was in some whore's bed, she was going to use one of his own fancy pistols on him.

She knew she didn't belong in a saloon, but he had left her no choice. Things had to change. If they didn't change soon, she was going to demand an annulment and go back east. Maybe Mrs. McBride could find her a different husband. She didn't know how she'd find the money, but she'd figure that out later. She could probably try finding a new husband in town, but she didn't think she could handle running into Tobias. Especially when he got remarried. Besides, who would want to marry her. They would probably all think there was something wrong with her. Why else wouldn't Tobias want her? There was nothing else she could do. She'd have to go back east.

She shook her head, nearly moved to tears. That wasn't what she wanted. She had taken an instant liking to her new husband. Despite how he had been avoiding her, she had managed to fall in love with *the idiot*. With his obvious love for his brothers, and the way he treated everyone else in his life, she knew deep down he was a very caring and giving person. He just didn't seem to care anything about *her*.

She stepped through the batwing doors of the saloon and couldn't help but shudder. She had come from a very gentle family. Her father had worked for the local bank. She wasn't used to men like the ones you found in an establishment made for carousing and drinking one's self into a stupor.

She clutched her hand over her rapidly beating

heart and gazed around the room, looking for her arrant husband. She spotted him across the overcrowded room at a table in the corner. He was sitting by himself with his head down. He had a bottle of whiskey, a third of it already gone, in one hand, and a glass in the other. She started across the floor, her gaze glued to Tobias, wondering why at this point he even bothered with a glass.

She was so absorbed with her thoughts, she didn't notice the big hairy, brute of a man before it was too late, and she was nearly running him down.

"Oh, sorry," she said, trying to move around him.

"That's okay," he said, grabbing her by the arm to pull her back around. "I know how you can make it up to me. How about a free tumble?"

"Sorry, a free tumble?" she asked in confusion. "What's that supposed to mean?"

"You know what I mean," he said, trying to wrap his arms around her. "I could use a good tumble, right now. I need something soft to sleep on for the night." He grabbed her bottom, squeezing her round cheek extremely hard, drawing a squeak from her. "You're a little over dressed for a saloon girl, ain't you."

She pushed hard in the middle of his chest, turning her face away when he tried to kiss her. "Let go of me. I think you've gotten the wrong idea. I just came in here to find my husband."

"Husband?" the man chuckled with a leer. "I can play your husband for the night if you want to play house," he added, wrapping his arms tighter around her, breathing in her face. His breath was very heavy with whiskey fumes, and the smell was making her feel faint.

"Tobias," she shouted, trying to get the blackguard's attention. "Let go of me, you drunken oaf."

"Now, let's not be that way. I'm sure I'm no different than any of the other men who've tumbled you."

"No man has ever *tumbled* me," she spluttered. "I just came in here after my husband."

"If you had a husband, you wouldn't be in here," he said, trying to bring his face closer to hers once again. Before he could though, someone latched on to the back of his old dirty coat, that looked like it should have been thrown out with the garbage a long time ago and swung him around causing him to release his hold on her.

She stumbled, nearly falling, before catching herself on the back of a chair. When she looked up, she found the dirty cowboy clutched in her husband's fist. "Keep your grubby hands off my wife."

"You? You're the husband she's so fired up about? No wonder she's coming to saloons for a tumble," the big brute said with a smirk. "You couldn't keep the first one happy. What made you think you could keep a second one happy?" he asked before wondering off with a chuckle.

Tobias turned his glare on Sadie, causing her to flinch. "Uh, Thaddeus told me where I could find you," she whispered, barely having the strength to say anything at all. When he just kept glaring at her, she wondered if he had heard her at all. "Maybe, I should go. I can see now, this was a bad idea."

Before she could take a single step, he grabbed her by the wrist and started dragging her to the door. "Really, Tobias, I'll go home. I can wait to talk to you, till tomorrow."

Once they made it outside, he stood there looking like he was looking for something. When he finally turned to look at her, his glare was only slightly less severe than it had been before. "Where's your horse?"

"I walked to town," she said, her chin coming up another notch. "Don't you remember my telling you in my letter that I have never ridden a horse?"

"You what?"

"I have never ridden a horse," she snapped, sounding exasperated.

"Never mind that. The other part," he growled back at her.

"I walked..."

He didn't let her finish. He turned his back on her and started heading down the street toward the livery stables, dragging her behind him once again.

"Tobias, please, slow down," she whimpered when she stumbled over a small stone in her path.

He stopped, turning back to her with a glare. Without saying a word, he bent and tossed her over his shoulder. He made it the rest of the way to the stables in just a few seconds.

When he stepped into the livery, the stable hand's eyes nearly bugged out of his head. "Good evening, Mr. Townsend. Is your wife alright? At least, I'm assuming that's your wife."

"You just pay no never mind, Jed Carter," he growled. "Get me my horse."

"Yes, Sir. Of course," he said, turning back toward the stalls.

"Don't go and sir me. I may be ten years older than you, but you played with my younger brothers growing up. Your father founded this town right along with mine."

"Yes, Sir."

"Jed," he snarled, giving him a stern look.

"I mean, Tobias," he nearly yelled, turning to take off in a run. "My parents only tried to teach me manners."

Tobias slid Sadie down his body, letting her land on her feet. Once the young stable hand returned, leading Gray Wind behind him, he mounted up, and without saying a word he yanked her up to lay across his lap in the saddle.

She landed with a grunt, shoving her hair out of her face, where it had finally fallen out of her bun, after her trip to town. "I can see you're going to be your usual, pleasant self."

He tipped his hat to the stable hand and lit out at a full gallop.

By the time she had bounced the nearly three miles back to the ranch house, she was ready to breathe fire. The second her feet hit solid ground again, she took a deep breath, ready to tear into him.

"Don't," he growled, handing the reins off to one of the ranch hands. He grabbed hold of her hand once again, dragging her up the porch steps and through the front door.

"Don't?" she nearly screamed, jerking to a stop, only managing to pull her hand free, because he was so surprised she was resisting him at that point. "You, don't. There was no reason to ride back here at a full gallop with me laying..." she huffed, coming to a stop. "You could have let me ride sitting across..." she growled, throwing her hands up in frustration, unable to find the words to finish her thoughts.

He glared at her, grabbing her hand once again, to drag her down the hall to his bedroom. He flung the door open, pushing her into the room before him.

"Why am I in here?" she asked with genuine confusion. "I figured this was the last place you wanted me to be."

He ignored her outburst, dragging her across the room to a chair sitting in the corner. He plopped down, yanking her across his lap on her stomach. When she felt him throw her skirt up over her head, she screeched at him. "What are you doing?"

"Giving you what you are obviously asking me

for," he said, yanking her knickers down around her ankles, exposing the round, pale globes of her bottom.

She gasped, trying to squirm off his lap. "I am not asking to be manhandled."

"Really?" he snorted, giving one full cheek a hard smack, causing her to scream. He ignored her protests, continuing on. "Then what do you think you were doing in that saloon?" he asked, giving her another hard smack. "I can assure you, if I had not found you when I did, you would have been far more roughly manhandled then what I'm doing right now. Jacob Daniels isn't known for his gentleness," he said with another swat.

"I was looking for you," she screamed at the top of her lungs.

"And another thing," he said, continuing to punctuate each statement with a swat to one of her cheeks. "You had no business going to town by yourself. Especially this late at night, and *especially* without a horse and wagon. What did you think you were doing? How did you think you were going to get back if you hadn't found me?"

By this point she was screaming so loud, he wasn't even sure she had heard him until she answered. "I would have just walked back."

That earned her another hard smack, before he jerked her off his lap, causing her to drop on her stinging bottom with a hard thump. "Ouch," she said, looking up at him with tears in her eyes. "Are you drunk?"

"No," he snapped. "I don't drink."

"Then what were you doing with that partially drank bottle of whiskey?"

"If I'm going to sit in the saloon, I am required to buy," he answered in an almost conversational tone. "It was partially drunk, because everyone in town knows I don't drink, and they all come by and get a drink. Basically, I buy everyone in the saloon a round of drinks."

"Do you pay for other... *pleasures* found in a place like that?" she asked, flushing scarlet.

"What?" he asked, his head snapping up. Was she asking what he thought she was?

She huffed, glaring up at him. "You know what I mean?"

By this point he was sure he did know what she meant, but he wasn't ready to tell her that. "Why no, my dear lady, I surely do not know what you mean."

She huffed again, pulling herself to her feet. "Where are you spending your nights? Whose bed were you sleeping in? I know you haven't slept here in the last three weeks."

"Are you trying to ask me if I've been sleeping with the whores?" he asked, raising an eyebrow.

She bit her lip, working to hold back the tears.

"Why? Are you jealous?" he taunted.

"I want children."

"There will be no children in this marriage."

"This is not a marriage."

"Marriage can be so many different things."

"This is not what God intended."

"Well, this is what it is."

She burst into sudden tears, turning her back on him. "I want an annulment."

He sucked in a really hard breath before standing to his feet. "No," he snarled before stomping over to the door.

She gasped, spinning around. "You can't stop me."

"Yes, I can. Even with an annulment, you have to get my consent and confirmation that you and I have not... Well, you know what I mean," he smirked.

"Anyone of your brothers could confirm that you

and I have not spent any time alone together," she said, crossing her arms with a huff.

"You want away from me bad enough to bring my brothers into this?" he snarled.

"You've given me no choice." She wasn't going to mention if he were willing to make theirs a real marriage, no one would ever be able to pull her away from him.

"If you push me, I'll do what I have to, to make sure you can't get that annulment."

"What's that supposed to mean?"

"Oh, I think you understand me just fine, on that point," he said, turning back to glare at her. "And I better not catch you in that saloon again, or what I just did will be mild compared to what I will do." With that said, he flung open the door and stormed out.

******

Tobias stepped out into the hall and punched the far wall, barely registering the crunch of his knuckles, before he realized his younger brother was standing there. "That was harsh."

"I wanted to make sure she didn't get the notion to visit anymore saloons."

"Not what I meant, and you know it. Don't you think threatening her like that was a little *barbaric*?" Cade asked, propping himself against the wall to block his brother from getting to the front of the house.

"She asked me for an annulment," he snarled, pushing past his brother, nearly knocking him to the floor.

"You've not really given her a reason to want to stay. She came out here with high hopes, believing she was marrying someone, who at least wanted a wife, even if she knew there was no guarantee he would ever love her. She didn't even get that."

"You know I didn't send for her. Thaddeus did."

"Then why did you marry her?"

"You know the answer to that, as well," he snarled once again, finally walking off, leaving his brother standing there.

"You are ruining the best chance you've ever had at happiness," Cade said, following behind him. "I warned you at the time, I thought marrying Rachel was a bad idea. You didn't listen then, and you are apparently not listening now."

"Don't talk to me about Rachel," he snarled.

Cade shook his head in frustration. "Don't let Rachel's memory ruin this marriage for you. It's not like you were even in love with her, but I think if you would just let yourself be, you could be with Sadie."

"Shut your mouth," he snarled, giving his brother a look that would deter almost anyone else.

******

Tobias stormed out of the house slamming the back door on his way, finally having lost his brother in the kitchen when he got distracted by the rest of the apple pie on the counter. By the time he had reached the barn, he was seething. He couldn't believe it. Once again, he found himself married to a woman who didn't want him, and this time was far more painful than before. Cade had no idea how right he was.

When he'd married Rachel, he hadn't married for love. He'd felt like he needed a wife. He had thought they needed a woman around the house for the same reasons Thaddeus had sent for Sadie. After Rachel's death, he had decided he would never marry again. He could manage with his brothers on his own.

That had been four years ago, when Wally, the youngest of them, was only eight and Thaddeus was twelve. He hadn't been dealing with babies, and Thaddeus was big enough to keep Wally out of trouble while the rest of them were working on the ranch.

While he hadn't been in love with Sadie when he married her, things were changing, very quickly. That had been one of the reasons he had been nearly in a panic, wanting to get her back on that stagecoach. He had known the moment he laid eyes on her, when she decided she was through with him, it would nearly kill him. Right now, he wasn't sure it wasn't going to kill him outright. There was no way he would survive watching someone else walk off with his beautiful Sadie.

He had been sulking around the barn long enough, he had started to calm down a little bit. Enough so, he could now hear the little voice at the back of his head trying to remind him, she had asked him for children first. It hadn't been until he had outright refused to give her any, that she had asked for an annulment. That didn't mean she was in love with him. Maybe if he agreed to give her children, she would stop fussing at him about an annulment.

He yanked the bedroll he had been using for the past three weeks down off the nail it was hanging from and walked over to the same empty stall he had been using to sleep in since she had arrived. He tossed it down over the fresh hay he had made sure to toss in there earlier and plopped down. He'd have to remember to wash it again tomorrow. He hadn't left the doing of it for Sadie. He didn't want to have to explain why it needed to be washed in the first place. He wasn't ready yet to tell her he had been sleeping in the barn for the last three weeks.

He wasn't sure what had made him want to lead

her to believe he had been bedding down with whores from the saloon. Maybe he had just wanted to see how she would react. She could ask any of his brothers, and they could tell her, he never touched the whores. It just wasn't something he was comfortable with. It went against everything he was raised to believe. Something he had continued to drill into his brother's heads after their father's death. Sex was supposed to be between a married couple.

If sex was supposed to be between a married couple, why wasn't he in there with Sadie, right now? Instead he was out here in the barn, tossing and turning, barely getting any sleep for the last three weeks. His brothers had made sure they were married. He just hadn't been able to bring himself to take advantage of that fact.

Honestly, he was just plain afraid, if he touched her the way he wanted, she would run from him like Rachel had, for sure.

Chapter 4
Saturday, April 10

Tobias stood from his chair, turning to leave. When Sadie rose to follow him, he shook his head, not bothering to make eye contact.

"Tobias, I would really like to talk to you," she said, following him, despite what he had tried to tell her with the gesture.

He shook his head again. "Not tonight," he mumbled, continuing through the door to the front room.

"If not tonight, then when?" she asked, just a step behind him.

Rather than answer, he opened the front door and continued outside, never looking back at her. She dipped her head, returning to the kitchen.

Cade gave her a concerned look. "Are you alright?"

She shrugged her shoulders, taking her seat. "I don't know," she whispered in answer. "I can't figure out what I've done wrong. Everything started out so well. I thought he at least liked me the day I met him. Now, I can't even get him to look at me, much less talk to me."

Cade shook his head. "It's nothing you have done."

She gave him a confused look. "How can you say that? He has barely spoken to me since our wedding day, and the times he has, it's been because I spoke to him first and wouldn't let him get away without doing so. And after that kiss..." she trailed off, turning a pretty shade of pink.

"He has things he has to work out, that have nothing to do with you."

"What kind of things?" she asked, biting her bottom lip.

Cade sighed. "Things I really shouldn't be the one to tell you about?"

She sighed, barely holding back the tears. "I would ask him, but he doesn't even stay around long enough for me to try."

Ezekiel, unable to take her sad look any longer, replied, "He made a serious commitment to a woman once. Things didn't end well."

She cocked her head to the side, giving him a pinched look, just feeling confused. "What do you mean, a serious commitment?"

"I really can't tell you anymore. You'll have to ask him," he said, giving her a sympathetic smile.

When he saw a tear slide down her pale cheek, he felt a strong urge to strangle his oldest brother. The man was throwing away what could possibly turn out to be the best thing in his life, if he would just give her a chance. He glanced over at Cade, begging for help with his eyes.

Cade sighed, and dropped his fork back to his plate, sitting forward in his chair, so he could prop his elbows on the table. "I don't know if any of us have told you, but when our father and little sister died, some of the ladies in town asked him if he wanted them to take Josiah, Thaddeus and Wallace to raise for him."

She glanced up, giving him a surprised look. "Why would they have done that?"

Cade shrugged. "He wasn't even twenty yet and had just inherited the largest part of the responsibility of running a very large beef cattle ranch. Of course, there were those that wanted to take the ranch over from us, as well."

She shook her head. "That doesn't really explain why they tried to take your little brothers."

"Sure, it does," Cade smiled at her. "They didn't feel like he could handle all of it on his own. They told him he wasn't much more than a child himself. Of course, if he had been a woman, they would have expected her to raise them."

She nodded, finally understanding what he was trying to say. "How old were the youngest three?" she asked, looking across the table at Josiah, trying to imagine him as a child. As large as the man was, that was very hard to do.

"Well, our father and little sister, Jolie, were killed in a carriage accident a little over eight years ago. It was in late January, and there was snow and ice on the ground," he said, thinking out loud. "Joe would have been twelve, Thad eight, and Wally was four."

"And they didn't think he could raise them? He had you other three for help. He didn't have to do it on his own."

"You are right," Cade nodded. "He didn't, and we have all worked together, including Joe, Thad and Wally, to make this ranch work, and to stay together. Unfortunately, Thad and Wally have had to grow up faster than most children, losing their parents so early in life. Josiah, as well, but I don't think it affected him quite as much."

She smiled across the table at the youngest two. "Well, I would say you have done a wonderful job working together," she said. "How did Tobias react to that? Besides the obvious. The obvious being, he kept you together."

"Well, he was not happy," Ezekiel laughed.

"That is quite the understatement," Cade said, looking very serious. "He called them all a bunch of interfering, busybodies, and told them to mind their own business."

She laughed softly. "Yes, I guess I can see him saying something like that."

Cade laughed with her. "Yeah, he told them he was going to keep our family together, and he did not appreciate their efforts to split us up."

"Yes," she nodded, tears starting to slide down her cheeks again. "That is one of the reasons I have already fallen in love with him. Because of how much love he obviously has for all of you. Knowing he is capable of so much love and commitment, makes me wonder what it is that is so wrong with me."

Cade sighed, realizing he had failed to distract her from her earlier thoughts. The other thing, as well, she had confirmed his suspicions with her confession of how she felt. She was already in love with his idiot brother, and the man didn't realize just how blessed he was. "Sadie, there is nothing wrong with you."

"Then why doesn't he want me?" she asked, bursting into tears.

Cade took a deep breath, wondering how much trouble he would get in, if he just beat the day lights out of his older brother. Considering, the only person he really would have to answer to *was* Tobias, made the thought all the more tempting. The only thing really stopping him, was the fear it would just upset Sadie that much more.

Cade sighed and leaned back in his chair. "I think he does want you," he said with an attempt at a reassuring smile. He figured his wanting her was the reason he took off after dinner each night. If he stayed around, where she was close, he knew he would end up giving into his desire to have her.

She gave him a hurt look, that said she thought he was cruel. "Why would you say something like that? Are you trying to make it more painful?"

He shook his head, trying to find the right words. "It all goes back to that serious commitment Ezekiel was talking about. He wants you, but he is afraid to admit it. Until he deals with those fears, he is going to keep running."

She turned her hands palms up and shrugged. "What do I do?"

"Unfortunately, right now, all you can do is wait."

She sighed, nearly being moved to tears again. "I guess I'll have to do as you suggest, for now."

"I wish our mother could have lived to be here with us," Ezekiel added. "She could give you better advice."

She dried her eyes and tried to smile. "What happened to your mother?"

Cade got a sad look in his eyes and whispered, "She died in childbirth when our sister, Jolie, was born."

She threw up her hands in frustration. "Until tonight, I didn't even know you had a little sister that had died."

"That was something else that was very hard on Tobias. Losing Jolie," Cade grimaced. "That's why the painting of her was taken down. So, he didn't have to look at it every day. There's a couple of photographs, but they have been stuffed in a drawer somewhere."

"Was he that close to your sister?" she asked, just wanting to understand the man she had married as much as she could.

"Well, it's a little more complicated than to say they were close. See, for a while, after Mom died, he had to take care of all of us, and run the ranch. Dad pretty much walked around in a kind of shock. It took him a while to get over our mother's death enough to take things back over. Jolie was about six-months-old when Dad finally asked Tobias what her whole name was, and who had named her."

"Tobias named your little sister, didn't he?" she asked, feeling shocked.

"Yes," Cade nodded. "He named her Sarah Jolene, after our mother. We called her Jolie from birth."

"He took care of your sister for those six months, didn't he?" she asked with a sigh. She had known he had a lot of love for his family. This had only confirmed that.

"Yes, he did," Cade nodded. "I think in a lot of ways, the things he has been through, has made him rather serious. And very wary."

She nodded her head, just trying to absorb everything they had said.

"There is another part to the story of my sister's birth."

She sat for a few seconds, just staring at the table, wondering what more there could be, before asking, almost afraid to do so. "What is that?"

"Those ladies that tried to take Joe, Thad and Wally, tried to get him to give them Jolie when she was first born. They told him she needed a mother to raise her, not a bunch of rough, ranchers."

"Offering help is one thing. Trying to take a child from their family is an entirely different one."

"They came back several times, trying to get him to change his mind. They used our father having so much trouble getting over Mom's death as a reason for him to give her up, as well."

She laughed. "I guess that didn't go over very well, either, did it?"

He gave her a big grin, shaking his head. "No, he called them a bunch of busybodies that time, too."

She sighed, drying her eyes once more. "I guess he has had a lot to deal with, in the last eight years."

Cade nodded his head, "Yes, so just give him time. He'll come around, even if *he* doesn't think so, right now."

She slowly nodded her head, getting up from her chair, to start clearing the table.

"Go on, and go relax, Sadie," Thad said, taking the stack of dishes from her hands. "We will do the dishes for you."

She gave him a smile, tears in her eyes, and mumbled, "Thank you," before turning to leave the room.

Cade waited till she was out of earshot before turning back to the others. "I think the luck of the Irish must have passed us all by."

Josiah nodded his head sadly. "It sure feels like it did."

Chapter 5
Thursday, April 22

Tobias stepped through the swinging doors, eyeing the room full of people, and wondered for what was likely the hundredth time, why he came here every night. He would sit in the corner, all alone, a bottle of whiskey in one hand, an empty glass in the other. He never drank the whiskey. He just sat there holding it, so the bartender wouldn't have him kicked out. The other patrons were so accustomed to his behavior at this point, they would leave the table in the back-corner empty for him, and then come by and refill their own glass with the whiskey in his bottle, every once in a while. Usually, by midnight, he would be out of whiskey, and ready to go home to his sleepless night in the barn.

He shook himself and made his way to the bar to make his purchase, before going to take his customary seat in the far corner. He raised his hand at the bartender without saying a word. The older man nodded his head, wiped a glass with his apron, and walked over to sit it down in front of him. He gave him, what could only be termed a confused look, and asked, "Tobias Townsend, why are you in here every night?"

He gave him a dirty look, grumbling, "Where's my whiskey?"

The old man shook his wrinkled jaws, his full, gray curls bouncing on his head. "You have a beautiful young wife at home," he chastised, a curious pain shining in his own eyes. "Why would you want to be here, sitting in the corner, supplying the town troublemakers with a couple of shots a piece. I know I wouldn't be here if I had something better to go home to."

He looked up, giving him a dirty look. "Mind your own business, Henry."

"That beautiful young lady is going to get tired of you running off to town every night. You'll be lucky if she doesn't leave you soon," the older man said with a shake of his head. "Mark my words. I've been there and lived to regret it. You will too, if you're not careful."

Tobias growled, leaning over the bar. "Once again, mind your own business, Henry. Where's my whiskey?"

He slammed the bottle down on the scarred-up wood of the bar and gave him a forced smile. "Here you go, Mr. Townsend. I sure do appreciate your business. You come again, now."

"Can it, Henry," he grumbled, getting up from his barstool to turn and walk away, taking his bottle of whiskey and empty glass with him.

He probably hadn't been sitting at his table five minutes, when the first of the bar patrons came by to get a free shot from his bottle. "Hey, if it isn't Tobias Townsend. The only man in town afraid of a little, tiny woman. So much so, that he runs off every night to sit in a bar all by himself."

When the man reached out to grab the bottle in Tobias' hand, he clamped down on it, not letting go. "Oh, come on now. What are you going to do with it? You sure aren't going to drink it."

Tobias looked up, finding the man doing all the talking only slightly familiar. He gave him an evil sneer, then tipped the bottle, filling his shot glass. He tossed the whiskey back quickly, not giving himself time to think twice about his actions and doing his best to ignore the burn.

The man chortled and shook his head. "Well, look here. I think Townsend has finally decided to be a man."

He wasn't sure what came over him. Without thinking, he poured himself another shot, and threw it back, knowing already, he was going to regret this the following day. He also missed, after the first shot, the bartender walking over to a door behind the bar and sticking his head in for a few seconds. Even if he had noticed, he wouldn't have known he had told the teenage boy that helped clean up after most of the patrons had left or gone upstairs with one of the girls for the night, to run out to the Townsend place and get one of the other Townsend boys to come and get their brother before he knocked himself out cold with whiskey.

By the time the man had finally gotten bored with harassing him, and had wandered off, he had drunk two more shots, and was feeling a little lightheaded. He was far gone enough, he wasn't even noticing it burning on the way down, anymore.

He was left alone for a little while, but eventually another one of the regular patrons walked over and managed to goad him into taking a couple more shots. If he kept this up, he was going to pass out, and slam his face into the table. His world was spinning out of control, and he wasn't sure he could make it across the room if he got up to leave. At this point, he was feeling fairly certain he would never make it up into the saddle.

He groaned, leaning his head against the wall behind him. He figured he was going to be spending the night right where he was.

He wasn't sure, because he could have been passed out for all he really knew, but he didn't feel like he'd had his eyes closed for very long, when someone else walked up. The sound of swishing silk was his only warning before someone plopped themselves down in his lap.

His left eye popped open and he glared at the woman sitting on him. "What do you want, Irene?"

She giggled, leaning into him, nearly smothering him with her cleavage, and whispered in an attempt at a sultry voice, "Well, I was wondering, since you decided to try the whiskey tonight, if you were feeling man enough to try *other* things, as well."

He pushed her back and growled. "Get off me. You know I don't want your services."

"The way you act, one wonders if you even have *working* equipment," she snorted loudly.

"I'm a married man. I just don't need your services," he growled, shoving her off his lap, or trying to, at least. The table was in the way and assisted her in staying right where she was. If he hadn't been so drunk, she wouldn't have been so lucky.

Irene snorted again. "I would be very surprised to find you had ever even touched that wife of yours once. After all, she hasn't run off yet."

"Get off me," he growled, shoving the table back and standing up, dumping her in the floor at his feet.

She landed with a thump, causing a large number of the drunken patrons to laugh and point. She stood to her feet and glared up a him. "How dare you?" she hissed.

"You're the one that walked up and sat down in my lap without an invitation. Maybe next time you'll wait till your asked," he smirked.

"Don't worry, I won't be *offering* again," she glared.

"That suits me just fine," he grinned, swaying on his feet. "Like I said before, I don't want your services."

She pulled herself up to her full five-feet four-inch height with a huff and turned to stomp off. He glared down at the table, trying to decide if he wanted to sit back down, or try to make it to the swinging doors. He was still standing there, trying to decide when he heard a very irritated voice coming from somewhere to the right of him. A voice he knew quite well. Even as drunk as he obviously was.

He glanced over, and grinned. "Hey, Brother. What are you doing here?"

"Henry sent a rider out to the ranch to tell me you were drinking your whiskey for some reason, instead of letting everyone else have it," he growled.

"Henry? Whose Henry?" he asked, nearly falling back into his chair and belching, breathing the fumes in Cade's face.

"Seriously? You don't even know the bartender's name?" he asked, giving his brother a dirty look. "After all the nights you've spent here in the last few weeks, I find that very surprising, even as drunk as you are."

"Oh, yeah. That's who Henry is. I knew that," he grumbled, taking a stumbling step forward.

"Whatever," Cade sighed. "Let's just get out of here and go home."

Cade followed behind him, barely resisting the temptation to kick him through the swinging doors.

Tobias stumbled outside, tripping off the boardwalk, to land sprawled out in the dirt, where he found himself staring at a dirty pair of boots. He rolled to his back, looking up a pair of very long legs, to finally stare into the eyes of another one of his brothers. "Hey, 'Zekiel. You came, too? What are you two doing in town this late at night?"

Ezekiel shook his head, frowning down at his oldest brother. "I could ask you the same thing? What got into your head, that you actually drunk the whiskey?"

Cade crossed his arms over his chest. "When I got in there, Irene was sitting in his lap. Thankfully, he dumped her out in the floor on his own, but this situation needs to be resolved, soon. *Real* soon. Do you catch my meaning?"

Ezekiel frowned, nodding his head. "Come on. Let's get him back to the ranch. Do you think he can stay in the saddle, as drunk as he is?"

Cade nodded his head. "He'll be alright. He could sleep in the saddle on that horse."

******

Tobias slid off his horse, falling to the barn floor. He groaned, rolling to his back, and tried to sit up. His head was still swimming too much, and he only made it about halfway before he fell back to the floor with a grunt.

"What do you think we should do with him? Dunk his head in the horse's water trough?" Ezekiel asked, eyeing his brother like he was a pile of cow dung.

Cade snorted. "I don't really want to do that to the horses."

"Well," Ezekiel sighed. "I guess we better take him in and give him coffee. Maybe we could dump a bucket of cold water over his head."

Cade grumbled under his breath, reaching down to yank his brother to his feet. "Come on. Get up, Toby. Mom would be devastated to see you like this."

Tobias stood to his feet, still a little wobbly, and gave his brother a dirty look. "That is not nice," he grumbled, referring to his brother's use of a nickname only his mother had ever used.

Cade smirked, knowing exactly what his brother was talking about. "What's not nice?"

Tobias shook his head, then groaned when his head started to pound. He closed his eyes, grabbing the front of Cade's shirt. "You know what I mean."

"Maybe I do, but you need to stop and really think about what you are doing, before you let it go any farther."

Tobias growled, giving him another dirty look, making sure not to shake his head this time. "There's nothing wrong with what I am doing."

Ezekiel snorted. "You have got to be kidding. You know darn well you are acting like a complete fool."

"No, I'm not," he said, forgetting not to shake his head. "Oh no, I think I'm going to be sick." He stumbled toward the open door of the barn, just managing to reach the outside before he threw up what was mostly whiskey.

He was still bent over, waiting for his head to stop spinning when his brothers followed him. "This is not something you would have ever done before," Cade said, stepping away, so he wasn't breathing in the smell of vomit. "Why are you doing this, now?"

"You know why." he grumbled, finally standing back up straight, finding that emptying his stomach had made him feel a lot better. His head had finally stopped swimming and he didn't feel so nauseated. He made his way back into the barn and headed for his bedroll and stall with fresh hay. He tossed his bedroll down, doing his best to ignore the other two behind him.

"You know, you have a much more comfortable bed inside," Ezekiel sighed, shaking his head. "You also have a very beautiful, and sweet wife in there who can't figure out why you don't even seem to like her. Why are you doing this?"

He grumbled once again. "You know why."

"No, we don't," Cade said, throwing his hands in the air. "Why won't you at least give her a chance?

You could at least take the time to get to know her."

Tobias shook his head, finding this time that it only made things a little blurry. "I am not going to let myself become attached to her, only to have her leave me the second she realizes she can't stand my touch, or to look at me. Or that she's afraid of me."

Ezekiel gave him a confused look. "Why would you think that was going to happen?"

"I know you heard Rachel shouting she wanted an annulment right before she ran off and broke her neck when she fell from that horse. Did I ever tell you, she left me a note explaining she had never wanted to marry me, in the first place? She said she couldn't handle the thought of me touching her. She wanted no part of the marriage bed." He knew that last little bit was just him adding to what she wrote, but that had to be what she had been thinking. *Why else would she have run the way she did?*

Cade sighed and shook his head. "I told you at the time there was something wrong with Rachel, and you should never have married her."

"Sadie came here to marry you, and expecting a normal marriage," Ezekiel added. "She isn't going to run off on you. Well, not if you actually give this marriage a chance, anyway."

Tobias shook his head. "I can't do it. I just can't," he grumbled, turning his back on them. "Please, just leave me be."

They both looked at each other, then watched as he crawled into his bedroll, and pretended they weren't both still standing there. They weren't giving up that easily, but they would let it go for tonight. They both figured they had browbeat him enough for the one night.

Chapter 6
Thursday, April 29

"Thank you, Mr. Miller. You have a nice day, as well," Sadie said with a smile at the older man and left the butcher shop while Jeremiah Miller held the door open for her. She stepped down off the boardwalk and placed the package she had in her hand in the back of the wagon, where Thaddeus waited for her. She turned back to take the other packages from Jeremiah, only to find he had stepped up beside her to place them in the wagon for her.

"Why, thank you, Mr. Miller," she said with a friendly smile.

"Please, call me Jeremiah, Mrs. Townsend. Mr. Miller is my father," he said, smiling back.

"I don't think I should do that," she shook her head, but softened the blow with a smile.

"You are probably right," he nodded, stepping back. "Your husband probably would not approve."

"Most likely not," she nodded before turning back to the wagon, taking Thad's offered hand for help up.

Before she could manage to step up into the wagon, Tobias reined Gray Wind to a stop beside the wagon and jumped down, out of the saddle. She noticed when his hat flew off, he must have just come from the barber shop across the street. His hair had gotten long enough it was curling around his ears, but now it was trimmed nicely, and lying flat against his temples.

He reached down to pick the cowboy hat up out

of the dirt and cram it back on his head, then started around the end of the wagon. She could tell by the furious expression on his face, she wasn't going to like what he had to say.

He stomped around to where she stood, and grabbed her hand, dragging her back around to where his horse was on the other side of the wagon. "Why are you..." he spluttered, before continuing. "Flirting with Jeremiah Miller?" he roared loud enough to gain the attention of several people walking down the street.

She gave him a hurt look. "I am not flirting with anyone," she replied, trying to understand what she could have done to make him react in such a way.

"That's not what it looked like to me, from across the street," he snarled, glaring back at the other man, who was now standing there, looking a little confused himself.

"Tobias, she wasn't flirting with Jeremiah. She was just thanking him for his help with the packages," Thaddeus said, trying to get his brothers attention.

"Stay out of this, Thaddeus," he growled, barely turning his head to look at his little brother, before turning to glare back at her some more.

"Tobias, calm down. We can talk about this at home," she said, doing her best not to cry.

"I will not have you flirting with every man in town," he growled, turning to stomp back over to where Jeremiah Miller still stood with his mouth hanging open. Before he managed to say a word, she threw herself up in Gray Wind's saddle. She sat the horse astraddle, not bothering to try to ride sidesaddle, the way his brother had taught her. Already feeling so humiliated over what her husband had said, she didn't give one thought to how high her dress tail was riding up. She turned the big horse in the direction she needed to go and headed back to the ranch.

"No, Sadie!" Thaddeus cried, just missing the reins of the horse when she slapped the horse across his rump with the leather straps.

Tobias jerked around in time to watch his tiny wife tear off, down the street on his very large horse. "Sadie, no!" he cried, starting out on foot. He had a fleeting thought of calling the horse back, but was afraid it would startle her, and she would fall out of the saddle and break her neck, anyway.

"Tobias," Jeremiah called, running up beside him. "Go down to the livery stables and tell Jed you need my horse. You can ride him bareback. He was trained by an old Indian friend of my father's. And he's the closest you are going to be able to come to being as fast as that horse of yours." Tobias nodded his head and took off without another word.

"Come on, Jeremiah," Thaddeus hollered. "We'll follow them in the wagon. Hopefully he'll catch her before she gets too far." He left the rest unspoken but, Jeremiah knew exactly what he was thinking.

******

Tobias made it down the street to the livery stable in record time. When he got there, Jed was already bringing Jeremiah's horse, Chance Lightening, out of the stalls. He had seen Sadie ride by on Gray Wind and had come out in time to hear someone holler to him what Jeremiah had said. He handed the reins over, not bothering with words, knowing the last thing Tobias was going to want to do was stand around and chew the fat. He stood watching as the other man climbed up on the horse bareback, and started out of town, sending up a silent prayer he managed to get to his wife before it was too late.

Tobias tore out of town, as fast as the horse would carry him. Which ended up being fairly fast. He never second guessed his direction, knowing Gray Wind would take her toward home.

By the time he had caught up to his wife on his horse, he was a nervous wreck. That might have accounted for the way he handled the situation. He rode up alongside Gray Wind and reached out and yanked her out of the saddle, right onto his lap.

He didn't realize he had been holding his breath for the last few seconds, until he took his first deep breath. Once he knew she was safe in his arms, and could breathe again, he slowed the horse and pulled back to look her in the eyes. When he saw her take a deep breath like she planned on laying into him with a verbal sit down, he clutched her to his chest and slammed his mouth down on hers. By the time he lifted his head, she was dazed and gripping his shirt in her hands.

He gave a sharp cry, slapping the reins against the horse's rump, aiming him toward the ranch. He clutched her to him, speeding the rest of the way home.

When he reined to a stop outside the house, he found Cade standing there with Gray Wind's reins. He wore a look crossed between concern and puzzlement.

When he saw them ride up, he smiled, taking a deep, relieved breath. "Thank God. I wasn't sure what to think when I found Gray Wind out here, rider-less. I don't think you've been thrown from a horse since you were about fourteen, when Dad gave you that palomino for your birthday. I don't think he was quite as big as Gray Wind, here. I remember Dad warning you not to get cocky with that horse, or he would end up teaching you a lesson."

Tobias lowered Sadie down to the ground, hopping off behind her. He wrapped Chance Lightening's reins around the porch rail, walking past his brother without a backwards glance, pulling Sadie along behind him.

Cade gave the big horse a strange look, just then realizing whose horse it was. "Why do you have Jeremiah Miller's horse?" he asked, following them into the house.

Tobias ignored the enquiry, continuing down the hall to his bedroom. He dragged her through the open door, slamming it closed behind them. Remembering the last time they had been in here together, she started struggling, trying to pull free, but to no avail.

He continued across the room, stopping at the chair in the corner. "Don't you dare," she screeched, yanking on her arm once again. He ignored her protest, yanking her down in his lap. When she felt him yank her skirt up over her head, she started struggling anew. "If you do this, I'll never speak to you again."

"From what I've noticed, you don't stop talking for long," he chuckled a mirthless laugh. "I figure you are going to find that rather hard to do." He proceeded by yanking her knickers down and giving her a solid smack on one full cheek.

"You are a brute," she screamed, her anger growing in leaps and bounds.

"Do not ever take off on my horse like that again," he growled, landing another solid smack.

She continued screaming, thrashing about, trying to get away. His grip on her hip held her firmly in place. "You have to be the meanest man I have ever met."

"I don't care how angry you are with me, or why you feel you need to leave. Stay off my horse, and any other horse my brother hasn't given you permission to ride," he continued, landing several more smacks to her bottom. "You have no business on a horse that large. It is dangerous."

By the time he came to a stop, he had given her several more smacks, the pale skin of her bottom was fiery red, and she had long since stopped screaming. She was now crying, tears pouring down her cheeks fast enough she was soaking his pant leg.

He sat there, still holding her across his lap, staring down at his handy work. This time when he let her off his lap, he gently stood her to her feet, making sure she didn't land on her abused rear end. He stood to his own feet looking down at her. "Do you understand me?" he asked in a much gentler tone than before.

She looked up at him, tears in her eyes. "Why don't you even like me? What did I do that was so wrong, you won't even give me a chance to show you I could be a good wife?"

He snorted, shaking his head, thinking about just how much he did like her. What she had done, was make him fall in love with her. "Stay off my horse," he growled, storming off toward the door.

"I want children," she pleaded, bringing him to a stop.

After a few seconds, he shook his head, snarling out, "No."

When he reached for the doorknob, she stopped him once again. "Then I want an annulment. I need something in my life to give me purpose."

"You have purpose," he snapped. "You take care of us." *And having you here keeps me from losing my mind.*

"That's not much purpose. Taking care of a bunch of men who were doing just fine taking care of themselves before I showed up," she huffed,

73

slamming her hands on her hips, her tears finally drying up, at least temporarily.

He shook his head, turning back to look at her. "Things are better since you got here."

"You couldn't prove that by the way you act," she retorted. "Besides, I want a husband who at least likes me. I want an annulment," she shouted, just before she burst into tears once again.

"No," he growled. "And if you don't let the matter drop, I'll fix it to where you can't get one."

"What's that supposed to mean?" she sniffled. "It's not as if you really want to touch me."

"You have no idea what I want," he grumbled, turning away from her again.

"You're right, I don't," she huffed. "Because you won't even talk to me, never mind actually tell me what you want."

You. "No more talk of an annulment. And stay off my horse," he growled, before finally leaving the room.

******

Tobias stepped out in the hall to find Cade standing there. "What do you want?" he snarled.

His younger brother shook his head at him. "This is becoming a bad habit of yours."

"She took off on Gray Wind," he growled, nearly giving into the temptation to punch another hole in the wall were his brother, Josiah, had just fixed the last one.

"I understand, she scared you, but you need to tell her why you don't want her on a horse bigger than Rosie," he said, crossing his arms over his wide chest.

"Scared me?" he shook his head. "She terrified me. I can't go through that again. And she asked me for an annulment again," he snarled, yanking on a handful of his hair. He couldn't even take the thought of losing her. Either to death, or an annulment. He wouldn't survive it, either way.

"Why won't you give her children?" Cade sighed. "It would make both of you happier. I know you always wanted children before."

"I didn't even want to be married," he snapped. "I wouldn't even have a wife if it hadn't been for Thaddeus sending for her. So, stop interfering in my decisions." That said, he turned and stormed off.

"I'll stop interfering with your decisions, when you start making the right ones," he whispered to himself, slowly following his pigheaded brother down the hall.

Inside the room, Sadie dropped to the bed with a thump when her legs buckled under her. "Oh, God. He never wanted me. That's why he avoids me like he does." She dropped her head to the beautiful, patchwork quilt and burst into tears once again.

******

Cade stepped out on the porch with a shake of his head. "If he doesn't let go of the past soon, he's going to run her off."

Thaddeus shook his head. "Maybe that's what he wants. Like he said, she wouldn't even be here if I hadn't sent for her," he sighed forlornly, dropping his head.

"No," Cade shook his head. "If she leaves him now, we won't be able to put his pieces back together. We'll lose him completely."

"I'm afraid we've pushed him too hard, already," Ezekiel added, looking sad.

"Maybe so, but unfortunately, we are going to have to see this through to the end," Cade nodded.

"It's the only way to make sure it works out. If we quit now, things could just go on like they are until she leaves. Or if we're lucky, she'll stay, but they'll grow old and never enjoy a *real* life together."

Thaddeus shook his head. "I'm afraid to push anymore. Earlier, if she had fallen off Gray Wind and broken her neck, it would have been enough to send him to the grave with her."

Ezekiel chuckled ironically. "I wonder if he even realizes he's already in love with her."

"Who knows. But either way, he's not going to admit it anytime soon."

"How much of that argument did Jeremiah hear, before he left?" Cade asked, looking concerned.

"Nothing, really. He was leaving by the time I came in," Thad answered with a shrug. "I don't see why it would matter. He would never say anything."

"It wouldn't really," Cade agreed. "But you know Tobias wouldn't want him to know any of this."

Chapter 7
Friday, April 30

The following morning, Sadie got up and started preparing breakfast as usual. She had been in there on her own for about half an hour when Thaddeus walked in with his head down. He plopped down in a chair, staring at the table. "You shouldn't have told Tobias you wanted an annulment."

She turned then to face him, unsure at first how to respond. After just a few seconds she answered, "You shouldn't have sent for a mail-order bride for him."

"How... Who told...," he stammered, the guilt staining his cheek. "We had all agreed you shouldn't hear about that."

"No one told me. I overheard Tobias and Cade talking about it after my fight with him, that you obviously overheard."

"He was married once before," he said, looking very sad. "I don't really remember her that well. She left him without really giving him a chance. She asked him for an annulment, just like you did."

She gasped, doing her best not to cry. "Is this the commitment Ezekiel was talking about?"

He nodded his head in answer, not really knowing what else to tell her. He was sure Tobias didn't want her to know about Rachel and how she had died.

"How am I supposed to know any of this?" she asked, throwing her hands in the air. "He won't talk to me. He avoids me like the plague. I'd be willing to try and make this marriage work, if he acted like he even half cared."

"He does care," Thaddeus said with a grin, thinking all would be well now.

"How can you know that?" she asked, crossing her arms in front of her. "You're the one that sent for me, not him."

"Oh, come on. We've all seen the way he looks at you," Ezekiel snorted from the door, causing her to jump nearly out of her own skin.

She clasped her hands over her heart, glaring at him. "When did you come in?"

He grinned ignoring her question. "He's just afraid you're going to leave him, like she did. And yesterday you gave him good enough reason to fear."

"Did all of you hear our fight yesterday?" she asked, feeling very vulnerable, not to mention embarrassed.

"Probably," he said with a grin. "I think you scared off every wild critter for miles around."

"It's hardly funny," she said, her cheeks firing up from the embarrassment.

"Maybe not," he said, trying not to laugh, "but it's obvious my brother cares for you very deeply."

"I doubt it. My bottom still... Anyway, it still stings," she said, blushing even more.

"Exactly. If he didn't care, he wouldn't have bothered. You put yourself in danger, riding his horse. That horse is too large and ornery for an *experienced* rider your size. And the only experience you've had is riding old Rosie. An old mare a three-year-old could handle without much trouble. You had no business even thinking about riding Gray Wind. Much less even doing it."

"Well, you should have heard what he accused me of," she huffed. "He embarrassed me in front of the whole town."

He shook his head. "Embarrassment is not a good enough reason to risk your neck that way."

"Ask Thad what he said to me," she said, pointing at the younger man.

Thaddeus shrugged. "It was bad, but not bad enough for you, someone who barely knows how to ride a much smaller, *slower* horse, to climb up on Gray Wind."

"Well, you're a lot of help," she huffed, eyeing her brother-in-law like a tiny, little bug she was thinking about squishing with the toe of her shoe.

"Besides, he only said it out of fear you're going to run off with someone else. He's terrified he's going to lose you."

She shook her head, still glaring at him. "I'm finding that hard to believe."

Ezekiel sighed. "This is the second time you have put yourself in danger."

"What are you talking about now?" she asked, pursing her lips."

"Your trip to the saloon," the two brothers said in unison.

"Well, I never did get to have the talk with him I wanted to have," she huffed.

"What did you want to talk with him about?" Ezekiel asked.

"Nothing. I don't want to talk about it with either of you two."

"Well, maybe you should talk to my hardheaded brother about it, then."

"That's what I was trying to do," she snapped, her anger rising. "Why else would I have walked all the way to town?"

"Okay." He took a step back, throwing his hands up in surrender, admiring her spirit. "If I can assure you that he will be here, in the house, tonight, do you think you can keep yourself out of trouble for the whole day?" he asked, trying not to laugh. She was a fiery one. If Tobias didn't straighten up soon, she just might skin him alive, and use his hide to make a rug. He only hoped when he decided to marry, he was lucky enough to find a wife with so much passion.

"How do you propose to keep him from running off, like he has done every night since our wedding day?" she asked, trying not to snap at him again. She knew he was trying to help, but she truly was at her wits end with her pigheaded husband.

"Let me worry about that," he grinned.

"Fine. I'll behave for the day," she said, pursing her lips.

"Good. No more talk of an annulment either."

"Fine," she snapped, glaring at him.

******

Tobias glared at his brother, then turned back to repairing the fence line. "What do you want?"

"Just to talk," Ezekiel said with a smirk.

"I don't feel like talking."

"Fine, if you don't want to know about Jeremiah Miller coveting your wife, I won't bother to tell you then," he said, turning his back on him.

Tobias spun around, a look of almost terror on his face. "What does it matter? She's my wife," he growled, grabbing his brother's arm. "No one touches her but me."

"It's not like you've actually touched her," Ezekiel pointed out.

"It doesn't matter," he snarled. "Jeremiah Miller better stay away from her. She's *my* wife."

"Yeah, well, I've been into town already today. He heard about her little trip to town the other night, and her visit to the saloon," he said with a grin, not bothering to add, he was the one that told him. "I wonder if he heard about her asking you for an annulment," Ezekiel pondered out loud with a smirk.

"She's not getting that annulment," he snarled, working to get his emotions under control. He really wanted to punch his brother in the mouth right then.

"Do you really plan on stopping her if she wants it that bad?" he asked, doing his best not to let his humor show. Sometimes it was just too easy to push Tobias' buttons.

"She's my wife."

"Then maybe you should treat her like a wife, instead of a maid." With that final bit said, Ezekiel turned, walking back toward the house. He knew Tobias would hang around after supper this time. The trap had been successfully set.

******

Sadie had just put the last bite of stew in her mouth when Tobias stood to walk around the table. "I need to speak with you," he said. She didn't even have time to panic, thinking he was leaving again, before he was pulling her chair out. He had startled her so bad, her last bite nearly went down the wrong way.

She looked up at him, swallowing before she spoke. "Uh, okay. I need to speak to you as well." She stood, feeling no less uncertain than she had for the last few weeks, and followed him down the hall to the parlor.

He opened and held the door, waiting for her to enter and take a seat. When she looked up at him, he cleared his throat and growled. "Have you been talking to Jeremiah Miller?"

"It would be a little hard for me not to. He is the butcher's son. He's always at the butcher shop. Why?" she asked, giving him a thoroughly confused look.

"Stay away from him," he snapped, glaring at her.

"How am I supposed to do that?" she asked, feeling even more perplexed.

"Thaddeus or Cade can take care of doing business with him," he grumbled, making it sound so reasonable. "You just tell them what you need and send them on their way. That's the way we did things before you got here."

"I thought my being here was supposed to make things easier on all of you," she said, giving him an irritated look.

"It still does," he growled. "Just do as I say."

"What about David Harris at the general store? Do I need to avoid him, as well? It's a good thing we have chickens and a milk cow. You might have someone else you want me to avoid," she snapped, rising to her feet and ramming her fists on her hips. "Oh, wait. I forgot about Jacob Peterson at the post office. Then there's the man at the livery stable in town. I don't remember his name. However, that's not really the point, is it?"

"You can stop with the sarcasm. Stay away from Jeremiah Miller, and just for good measure, all the rest of them, as well," he growled, stepping closer. "Young and old, a like. Married or not."

"The way you're acting, I'm surprised you let me talk to your brothers," she said, giving him an almost hurt look. "Am I not allowed to talk to anyone else?"

"Just stay away from any man not myself or my brothers."

"Why?" she asked, throwing her hands in the air.

"Because, you're not getting that annulment, I don't care how bad you want it," he snarled crowding her even more.

"You don't know the first thing about what I want," she snapped, tears springing to her eyes.

"What's that supposed to mean?" he asked, remembering last night when they'd had this conversation in reverse.

"Figure it out for yourself. I'm tired. I'm going to bed." She turned to walk toward the door but was stopped short.

"You're right, you are," he said, yanking her back around and tossing her over his shoulder.

She screeched, pounding on his back. "Put me down, you big brute. What are you doing?" He stormed through the door and started down the hall.

"Man, what are you doing?" Ezekiel asked, giving him a confounded look.

"Taking my wife to bed. What does it look like I'm doing?" he snapped, snarling at his brother this time.

"Digging that hole *a lot* deeper, that's what," Ezekiel said with a shake of his head. "This isn't the way to go about this, Tobias."

Tobias just ignored him, continuing on to his room, slamming the door behind him. He tossed her to the bed, giving her a devilish look.

She screeched, trying to roll out of the way, but she was too late. She squirmed and tried to push him off when she found him lying over her. "What are you doing?" she asked, feeling a little nervous swirl in her stomach.

"Claiming my rights as your husband," he growled just before slamming his mouth down on hers.

The kiss may have started out hard and demanding, but it wasn't long before it gentled and he started coaxing her to participate. The moment she felt the change in him, she moaned, and melted into him, wrapping her arms around his waist as tightly as she could, not knowing what to do, other than to hang on. It wasn't long before her anger was completely gone, along with all their clothes.

Chapter 8
Saturday, May 1

Tobias walked into the kitchen in the best frame of mind he had been in since meeting his beautiful wife over three weeks ago. His jolly mood only lasted long enough for his brother to make it to the kitchen behind him. He was frowning, and Tobias could tell he had something to say, he wasn't going to want to hear. He did his best to ignore him, continuing with his breakfast preparations.

He poured himself a cup of coffee and carried his plate to the table, while doing his best to disregard Ezekiel's obvious irritation. He sat down and picked up a piece of bacon and started to eat like he was the only one in the room.

"Man, what were you thinking last night?" Ezekiel snarled, finally breaking the silence. He pulled out the chair directly across from his brother and dropped into it with a thump.

"I don't know what you are talking about," Tobias answered without looking up.

"Really? Is that what you're really going to use as your defense this morning?" he snorted back. "Where's Sadie? Why isn't she fixing breakfast this morning?"

"Still in bed, asleep," he said with a small smile Ezekiel almost missed when he still didn't look up from his plate of eggs and bacon.

"Is she okay?" he asked, finally provoking him enough to get him to look up.

"Of course, she is. Why would you suggest

otherwise?" Tobias snapped back, staring his brother in the eye.

"You have to ask after what you did last night?" Ezekiel asked, sitting back in his chair to cross his arms over his massive chest.

"I didn't do anything wrong last night," Tobias growled. "I have no idea what you are even talking about."

"Sure, you do. You pretty much forced yourself on her."

"No, not even close," he snarled, sounding like an old bear somebody had poked in the eye with a stick.

"You carried her down the hall like a sack of potatoes," Ezekiel stated, raising an eyebrow.

"If she had truly resisted, I would have stopped," Tobias snapped. "You should know me well enough to know that. I would never hurt a woman, especially not her. She didn't offer any resistance at all. I did not force her," he growled, barely resisting the urge to punch his brother in the nose.

Sadie picked that moment to enter the kitchen. Both brothers could tell by the look on her face, she had heard the largest part of their argument. After all, they hadn't exactly been whispering. Tobias had gotten loud enough to raise the roof off the rafters.

The immediate, dead silence was deafening after the last couple of minutes of shouting. Sadie and Tobias stood staring at each other, flushed to the roots. Ezekiel shook his head and turned toward the back door. "I have work to do. The fence around the north pasture needs repairs. I'm going to take a couple of ranch hands with me, but I'll leave you Wilson. I remember you saying something about needing to send him into town for supplies. I'll see you both at lunch time. *I hope*," was mumbled under his breath as he stepped out onto the back porch.

Sadie watched as the back door slammed shut

behind Ezekiel, then turned to face Tobias. She wondered if he had heard what his brother had mumbled on his way out the door. She just hoped he didn't bring up what happened last night. As much as she had wanted it to happen, she didn't think she was ready to talk about it.

"I'm sorry I overslept," she said, blushing prettily.

"No apology needed," he grinned warmly. "I deliberately let you sleep in. I know I didn't let you get much sleep last night," he said, testing the waters.

"I don't want to talk about that," she said, dropping her head and walking over to the sink.

"Why not? We're married," he snorted, giving her back a dirty look.

"Yes, we are," she sighed "But I still don't really know where I stand with you. Have you eaten breakfast, yet?" she asked, trying to change the subject.

"Yeah, I ate. Those are my dishes on the table," he growled. "Just remember what I said last night. Stay away from the men in town."

Sadie waited till she heard the door bang closed behind him before she spun around and dropped into one of the chairs. She was so emotionally raw from all of it, that when Cade walked in and asked how she was feeling, she promptly burst into tears.

"Hey now, it can't be all that bad, can it?" He knelt down in front of her to take her hands in his.

She shook her head, refusing to look up at him. "I really hoped our getting married on Saint Patrick's Day was a good omen, but I guess I was out of luck."

"Just hang in there. He'll come around."

"He doesn't want me to go to town for supplies," she sniffled, wiping her eyes with her fingers. "I'm supposed to send one of you. What does he think I'm going to do?"

Cade gave her a guarded look. "He's been married before."

"I know about that," she huffed, giving him a dirty look. "Thaddeus told me. What I don't know is, what happened to her, and what it has to do with me."

Cade sighed, standing back to his feet. "It's not my place to tell you. You're going to have to ask Tobias about it."

"Great, ask Tobias," she huffed sarcastically. "Tobias doesn't talk to me. Last night is the most he's talked to me since we got married. And that was only so he could tell me to stay away from *all the men in town*," she growled, waving her hands in the air over her head in frustration. Her mind immediately went to what happened after, and she turned red from embarrassment. She ducked her head, avoiding eye contact.

Cade stepped back, trying not to let her hear him chuckle. He knew what that blush was about. They all did, but he didn't want to embarrass her any more than she already was.

She shook her head and rose to her feet. "I have a list of supplies I need picked up from town."

Cade nodded, understanding her need for a change of topic. "That's fine. Wally and I can go into town as soon as breakfast is done."

"I'd really like to go," she sighed forlornly. "I would like to get some fabric to make a couple of new dresses," she said in explanation. "I don't know how he expects me to get things like that, if I'm not allowed in town. And I've not really had the chance to ask."

"I'm sure you're allowed in town. He just doesn't want you deciding to run off with another man," Cade said with a chuckle.

Sadie just looked stricken for about two seconds

before bursting into tears again.

"Okay, that was my enormously, *obviously*, failing attempt to make you laugh," he said, patting her on the shoulder. "I won't be doing that again."

******

After finally eating breakfast with the rest of his brothers and Sadie, Cade went looking for Tobias. He found him in the barn. "You need to let Sadie go to town. She has some things she needs for herself. I don't want to be responsible for picking them out. I don't figure any of the others do, either," Cade huffed, doing his best to school his features so Tobias didn't detect his humor.

"I never said she couldn't go to town," Tobias answered, not bothering to turn around, as he continued with the task of feeding the horses still in their stalls.

"Well, that's the impression she got after what you told her last night." Cade crossed his arms over his chest, eyeing his brother. Despite he and Sadie's obvious argument last night, he seemed to have a lighter spirit this morning. Things were *definitely* still rocky, but there was finally some hope shining through.

"I never said she couldn't go to town. I only said one of you had to deal with picking up supplies," he answered, finally turning his head enough to look at his brother, before going back to his task. "What does she need to go to town for, anyway?"

"She wants fabric to make herself some new dresses. And you need to explain to her what you meant, because she's in there crying her eyes out, as we speak."

Tobias spun around and gave his brother a dirty look. "You know, you could have just said that."

"Well, I just did," Cade said, rubbing a hand over his mouth to hide his huge grin.

"No, you wrote a book first. Next time, just get to the point," Tobias snarled, stomping toward the barn door.

"Hey, where are you going? There's work to be done," he said, barely holding back a chuckle.

"Then get it done," Tobias snapped back. "Have Wilson help you. I'll get any supplies we need from town."

"Well, where are you going?"

"To take my wife to town," Tobias snarled. If he had turned back, it would have been to find Cade nearly bent over double and red faced from holding in the laughter. Tobias could deny it all he wanted, but he was already in love with his beautiful new wife.

******

Sadie jumped and spun around to see who was coming in the back door. When she saw the scowl on Tobias's face, she spun back around, not wanting him to see how red her eyes were, from crying.

"You need to be ready to leave by the time I get the horses hitched to the wagon," he huffed, just wishing she would look at him.

Sadie gasped and had to fight not to start crying again. "I thought one of your brothers was going to take me."

"If you're going to go, I'm going to be the one to take you." He stormed back out the back door, much the same way he had entered it not a full minute before.

Sadie stood there in a state of shock wondering what this meant. Did it mean he genuinely cared, or was he afraid someone else would try to take her away from him? Currently, she felt more like a piece of property, and less like a wife. So far, the only time she had felt like more than a possession was last night, while she was in his arms. Last night she had felt loved.

It wasn't ten minutes later, and Tobias came back in ready to go. Sadie jumped up from the chair where she still sat contemplating her situation. "That was fast. I figured you would be gone longer."

"Cade had already gotten started by the time I got back out there. I helped him finish," Tobias said in the closest he'd come to a conversational tone with her since they had married. He had decided while he was outside to try and have a pleasant day with her today. He knew if they had any chance of making their marriage work, he was going to have to start showing her a little of the feeling he held in his heart, and less of the thoughts he held in his head. He had to constantly remind himself, it wasn't her fault what his first wife had done.

"Oh. Well, I guess I'm ready then," she said, walking toward the door.

"I thought you would want to change your dress," he said, a little puzzled. "I can give you a few more minutes."

"I really don't have much to choose from. I have this dress and one other for work around here," she shrugged, blushing to her roots, even though she knew she had nothing to be embarrassed about. "Then the one dress I save for Sunday to wear to church."

When she turned back toward the door once again, he stopped her with a hand on her arm. "Are you telling me, you only have three dresses?" he asked, sounding incredulous.

"Yes," she whispered, dropping her head. "That's what I'm used to. My mom helped me make a couple new ones before I left to come out here. The everyday dresses I had at the time were way too ragged. It was embarrassing enough coming out here with so little."

Tobias put a gentle hand under her chin and lifted her eyes to meet his gaze. "You have nothing to be embarrassed about. I wish you had said something sooner."

"That was really difficult when you were doing your best to ignore me," she said, tears in her eyes.

"Please, don't cry. In the future, if I'm being difficult, and you need something, you have my permission to ask one of my brothers for help," he said with a self-deprecating grin. "They'll be happy to knock some sense into me, for you."

She gave him a watery smile and sniffled. "Thank you."

"Will you tell me where you came from? Tell me what brought you out here?" he asked, turning her toward the door to lead her outside.

"Are you sure you want to know?" she asked, giving him a shy smile. "It's kind of boring."

He shook his head. "Oh, I doubt anything about you could bore me."

When they reached the wagon, they both fell silent for the time it took him to help her up in the seat and then follow her up. He turned it toward town, then tried again. "Will you tell me, please."

"Well, I came from New York," she started.

"That much I did know. That's all Thad told me before I came to pick you up at the Stagecoach that day. He didn't say anything about family you might have left behind, or if you had any family at all."

"All I have left is my mother," she said, tears filling her eyes. "I was an only child, and my father died two years ago."

"I'm sorry. I don't want to make you cry, but I really want to know," he said, giving her an encouraging smile.

"It's alright," she said with a sniffle. "I just miss my mom."

"So, she's in New York, with no family left near her?"

"Yes," she said, bursting into tears for the third time that morning, and it wasn't even past eight yet.

"Sadie," he said, wrapping an arm around her. "Please, tell me what's wrong."

"When my father was alive, we were used to a better lifestyle. Not rich by any means, but better," she said, wiping her eyes with her fingers. "He worked at a bank. He had built up a pretty good savings before he died. My mother and I had been living off that savings for the last two years. That's why I came out here with so little. We've been trying to make it stretch. At first, we tried to find work. There just wasn't anything. At least not anything that didn't involve my losing all my moral standing," she added with a blush. "It was my mother's idea for me to become a mail-order bride. She even went to Mrs. McBride's with me. I don't know if I could have gone through with it if it hadn't been for her moral support."

He gave her a concerned look, already trying to work out a way to bring her mother out here with them. "Are you saying she's almost out of the money she needs to live on?"

"Yes," she said, sounding like she was about to burst into tears, yet again. "At least we didn't have to use any of her savings for me to get out here. You sent... Well, Thaddeus sent enough for me to make the new dresses and pay for my train ticket, then stage fair. I even had a little money left to eat with on the train. When I got off the stage, my last meal had been almost sixteen hours before. I thank God Thaddeus sent me as much as he did."

"Yes, thank God for that," he mumbled under his breath, shaking his head. *He had to have sent it out of his own stash, or I would have noticed.*

By the time they had reached town, Tobias had made a decision. As soon as he got back to the ranch, he was going to ask Thad for the information to contact Mrs. McBride. He was going to get Sadie's mother out here with them. Before she starved to death. He wasn't going to ask Sadie if he could avoid it. He didn't want to get her hopes up, just in case they didn't get to her before it was too late.

******

Tobias opened the door to Harris General Store, then stepped back and motioned for Sadie to enter ahead of him. "Hello, Mrs. Harris," he greeted the older woman at the front counter. "How are you doing on this fine April morning?"

"Well, if it isn't Tobias Townsend and his young bride," she said, stepping around the counter. "I'm doing wonderful today. How about you all?"

"We're doing pretty good. We have some supplies we need to pick up," he said, handing her the list Sadie had wrote out earlier. "Sadie was wanting to get some material to make her some new dresses, as well."

"Well, if you want to, go right ahead and start looking at the fabric over there and I'll get David to start filling this list. Then I'll be right over there to help you."

"Thank you, Ma'am," Sadie said with a nod of her head.

Once Mrs. Harris and David came out of the back of the store, she headed to the front where Sadie was already looking at a bolt of fabric. Tobias stopped her when she went to pass by him. "Make sure she gets at least enough fabric for three dresses. At least one of them needs to be a Sunday dress. If she shows interest in more than that, get it all. Make sure she gets anything else she needs. Don't worry about the cost. She came out here with three dresses. If she fusses with you, set it back and get it while she's not looking."

"What about shoes and bonnets?" the older woman asked with a huge smile.

"Whatever she wants, or you feel is needed that she's not asking for. I'm going to leave it in your capable hands. You know, I know nothing about women's clothing."

"You know something, Tobias Townsend?" she asked with a very motherly look. "This is the most I've heard out of you at one time in the last four years. That young lady is going to be good for you yet."

"I think you're right, Mrs. Harris," he said with a grin. "*I think you are right.*"

He watched as she finished making her way across the store, then turned back to where David was already laying out some of the supplies on his list.

"Good morning, Tobias. Did you enjoy your trip in this morning? This weather sure is nice for this time of year. It's usually still a little on the cold side, this early in the morning."

"Yeah. Lots of Easter lilies along the road. Sadie really enjoyed them."

"She sure is pretty, your Sadie."

"I quite agree with you," Tobias said with a smile as he watched his young wife. "I'm going to head over to Miller's. I should be back before they are done, but if I'm not, would you mind telling Sadie where I've gone?"

"No, I think I can do that for you," David said

with a grin. "You have a good day, now."

"You, as well," Tobias said on his way out.

******

"Good day, Mr. Miller," Tobias said with a nod of his head. He already had what he needed and was turning to leave when Jeremiah, the owner's son, walked in.

"Hello, Tobias," Jeremiah said with a friendly smile. "I just saw your wife over at the general store. She is quite fetching. You really got lucky."

"Stay away from my wife," Tobias snarled, wanting to punch the other man in the face.

"Hey, take it easy, Tobias. I just said she was fetching. I haven't got any plans of trying to run off with her," Jeremiah said, taking a step back.

Tobias took a step forward with a snarl. "I was told you wouldn't mind marrying her yourself."

Jeremiah nodded his head, raising an eyebrow. "What man interested in marrying wouldn't. She's very beautiful, but I said that when she first got here. Before you were married. I had heard you really didn't want to marry her."

"Well, we are married," he snapped. "And we're going to stay that way. So, don't be getting any ideas about my wife."

"Tobias, I would never try to take another man's wife," Jeremiah said, crossing his arms in front of him, finally sounding both irritated and hurt. "You should know me better than that. You've known me all my life. We went to church together. Got in trouble together at school more times than I can count."

"Yeah, I know," he said, shaking his head, and taking a step back. "I'm sorry. I'm just a little wound up. We've had a rough start."

"Hey, I get it," he grinned. "How did everything with her ride on Gray Wind go yesterday? All I know is, you got to her before she got hurt."

Tobias flushed, remembering his reaction might have been a little extreme. "I am fairly certain she will not be getting on such a large horse, ever again."

"That's good," he nodded. "Maybe you should explain to her what happened to your first wife."

"I don't want to talk about Rachel," he snarled.

"Okay, I'm sorry. Do you mind telling me where Sadie came from? Maybe I could get me a mail-order bride. There's a definite shortage of single, marriageable women around here," he said with a grin. "The ones that are around here, I've known since they were in pigtails. They're too much like sisters to me."

"You'll have to ask Thad about it. He sent for her. I'm starting to really feel grateful to him for that," Tobias whispered to himself as he turned to leave the butcher shop.

Chapter 9
Monday, May 3

Tobias had made his way to the kitchen right alongside his beautiful wife. Thankfully, this morning turned out to be one of Thaddeus' early mornings. He was only sixteen, and there were times when he or Cade had to go in, and pretty much toss him out in the floor. This morning, however, he was in the kitchen before Sadie even made it there.

The moment Tobias seen him, he understood why he was up so early. His stomach had driven him out of bed. He was sitting at the table, already snacking on a biscuit left over from yesterday, with two more sitting on a plate in front of him. He remembered mornings like that when he was growing up. There were just times when a teenage boy just couldn't get full enough. He recalled times, sitting down at the dinner table, and eating two or three plates full of food before he would even start to slow down. Then he would still end up eating dessert, as well.

"Hungry, I see," he said with a deep chuckle. Thaddeus looked like a momma lion guarding her cubs, the way he was protecting those biscuits.

"Ha-ha. I'm starving," he grumbled. "Do you want help cooking breakfast, Sadie," he asked in a much lighter tone.

"Just eat your biscuits, Thad," she said, patting him on the shoulder as she made her way to the counter.

Tobias waited till Sadie went outside with the egg

basket to collect eggs from the chickens for breakfast, before turning to his little brother. "Thad, I need the information for the mail-order bride service that sent Sadie out here," he blurted, praying he didn't have to offer a real long explanation. He didn't want her to know what he was up to yet.

His little brother all but stuck his bottom lip out and gave him a belligerent look. "You're not sending her back, Tobias. The rest of us already love her. She's wonderful."

He shook his head like he thought his little brother had lost his mind. "I have no intentions of sending her back."

Thaddeus continued like his older brother hadn't even spoken. "Besides, how would you feel, if you found out years from now, you sent her away pregnant, and you had a child."

"Thad, I'm not sending her away," he said, taking a seat across from him.

"Then why do you want that information?" he asked in puzzlement.

"I wanted to see if they could help locate her mother. I want to bring her out here before she starves to death. Or ends up on the streets. From what Sadie told me, I don't have much time."

Thaddeus' eyes grew huge. "She could starve to death?" he asked, looking down at the biscuit he held in his hand, then at the one left on the plate. "That would be a horrible way to die."

"Yes, it would be," he nodded. "They were almost out of the savings her father left them when he passed away. That's the reason she became a mail-order bride. Her mother wanted her to get married, so she wouldn't have to do something *horrible* to survive," he added, wanting to avoid giving any more details than that.

Thad nodded his head in understanding. "Her

mother didn't want her to have to go to work in some saloon."

"Yeah," he said, giving his brother an annoyed look. "That was the part I was trying to avoid saying. I didn't think it was necessary."

"Oh, sorry," Thaddeus said, finally feeling embarrassed, and blushing to his roots. But not embarrassed enough to stop him from eating, as he started on his last biscuit.

"Never mind that," he said, waving his hand in front of him. "Thankfully, Sadie was an only child, but it leaves her mother out in New York, by herself. They didn't have any other family."

"Oh, we definitely need to move her out here with us," Thaddeus agreed. "That will make Sadie very happy."

"Don't say anything to her yet," he added with a very serious look. "We have no idea if we'll ever find her, or what condition we'll find her in. I don't want her getting her hopes up."

Thaddeus nodded his head in understanding, looking very serious himself, still chewing on what had to have been half of a biscuit.

"Do you still have the information?" Tobias asked, trying to prod his brother out of his early morning stupor.

"Sure," he said, jumping up, intending to go for the information right then.

Tobias grabbed his arm. "Hang on. Wait till after breakfast. Then bring it out to the barn to me. I don't want her to see you handing me anything. I don't want her wondering what I'm up to."

The young man sat back down with a nod. "Okay."

Just in time too, because the second his rear end hit the chair, the door opened, and Sadie came back in carrying the eggs she had collected. She eyed the two still sitting at the table, wondering what they were up to. "It won't take me long and I'll have everything going. Do you want more biscuits with the eggs and bacon, this morning?" she asked Thaddeus, sitting her basket on the counter.

"Sure, that sounds great," he answered, hopping up from his chair. "Do you need help?"

Tobias stood up, doing his best not to look at his wife too closely. "I'm going to go ahead and get started. I'll be back in an hour for breakfast. Thad, why don't you go and milk the cow, so Sadie doesn't need to. I'm sure that would be a big help,"

Sadie nodded her head. "Yes, that would be a great help. I'm still not comfortable with milking Miss Daisy. I don't think she likes me much."

"It's not that she doesn't like you," Thaddeus grinned. "She can sense that you are nervous. It makes her nervous, too."

******

Tobias pulled the wagon to a stop, eyeing the broken fence. From the look of things, that ornery, old bull had been charging it again. "How much longer did you say it was going to take for John Wilson and his group to get the rest of the new barbed wire fence up? I'm getting tired of having to fix these wooden ones, after Festus gets done with them. Maybe the barbed wire ones will stop him."

Ezekiel shuddered, nodding his head. "I know it would stop me. I wouldn't want to run into that stuff."

Tobias nodded his head, shooting his brother a deceptively, serious look. "Well, there's some hope then. You've got about as much good sense as that ornery, old bull does," he said, never showing even a hint of a smile.

The younger man slapped his knee and chuckled. "Wow, someone's feeling on top of the world this morning."

Tobias just shook his head. "Well?"

"Well, what?" his brother asked, giving him a confused look.

He just sighed, trying not to let himself get irritated. "How much longer is the fence going to take?"

"Oh, I think he said it should take about two more weeks."

He nodded. "You did say this pasture was empty, for now, right?"

His brother chuckled, his grin growing huge. "Yeah, Festus has been moved over to the far end," he answered, pointing to the south.

"Good," he grumbled, finally hopping down from the wagon.

"You're still afraid of old Festus, aren't you?" Ezekiel chuckled.

"I'm not afraid of that old bull," he denied, turning red. "I just don't like him much."

"Sure, you're not," his aggravating brother chuckled again.

He sighed, deciding it was best just to let it go. "Come on. Let's get this fence fixed. I've got to go into town and send a wire."

"Who are you sending a wire to?" Ezekiel asked, hopping down from the wagon with his brother.

"To a Mrs. McBride," he answered, not wanting to reveal anything else.

"Who is Mrs. McBride?" he asked, crossing his arms to give his brother a hard look. If Tobias was up to what he was thinking he was, he might just try his hand at beating some sense into him.

"Don't worry about that right now," he said, turning back to the wagon, to start unloading supplies. "We need to get this done. I've not got time to talk."

"Well, you're going to make time," his stubborn brother declared. "Or I'm just going to keep standing here."

"Fine," Tobias growled, turning to toss the lumber they had brought with them down by the broken fence. "If you must know, she is the lady that sent Sadie out here."

Before he knew he was going to do it, when Tobias turned back, Ezekiel punched his older brother right in the mouth. He was so shocked, he just shook his head, and stood there staring back at him at first. That shock was probably what saved Ezekiel's hide.

"What was that for?" he grumbled, rubbing his jaw, still wondering what was going on.

Ezekiel growled, stepping closer to his idiot brother and cracked his knuckles, like he was thinking of punching him again. "Why would you need to send a wire to the lady who sent Sadie out here? And I would think very carefully, before I answered, if I were you."

"Don't get the idea you'll get away with that a second time," Tobias snarled at his brother, before finally sighing. "How else am I supposed to find Sadie's mother, and have her sent out here before she starves to death."

"Sadie's mother could starve to death?" Ezekiel asked, forgetting his anger fast enough, he didn't even think to relax his hand from the fist he still had it in.

"Yeah," Tobias nodded. "Were you thinking I was going to try to send her back, like Thaddeus was when I asked him for the information to contact the lady?"

"Well..."

"I know," he sighed, shaking his head. "I haven't exactly given you all a reason to think I wouldn't try to."

"You know, married life seems to agree with you," Ezekiel grinned. "You've been happier the last couple of days, whether you're ready to admit it or not."

"Now you just sound crazy," he snorted.

"You're seriously going to try and deny it?"

"I'm just trying to make the best out of what I've been handed."

"Right? That's what you call *sleeping* with her every night? Just making the best of it?"

"Don't get too excited," he said, glaring back at him. "I'm just trying to give her that baby she wants. Then I'll move her back to her room."

"Why?" his brother asked, throwing his hands up in the air. "You're trying to spite us, and you're spiting yourself."

Chapter 10
Thursday, May 13

Tobias and Sadie had just finished eating lunch at the café, where he had promised they would eat when they came into town for supplies. He held the door open, and waited for her to exit, thinking about how beautiful she looked today. She gave him a shy smile, before stepping out onto the boardwalk to take his arm. She wore one of her new dresses, she had made from the fabric she had gotten from Harris' General Store. It was a peach color, trimmed in white, and brought out a rosy glow to her cheeks. He wondered at how she seemed to grow more breathtaking with each day.

He smiled down at her, giving her a reassuring pat where her hand rested at his elbow. "Did you want to go to see if Mrs. Martin had any dresses already made you could use for every day. I still need to check in with Mr. Taggert to see if he has that order for Thad ready."

She gave him a hurt look, tears welling up in her eyes. "Do you not like my new dress?"

He gave her a soft smile, wondering how long it was going to take for her to be as comfortable with him as she was the day they met. "Yes, Sadie, I like your new dress. You look beautiful. I just thought you would like to get some everyday dresses that were already made, so you don't mess up your lovely dresses while you are cooking and cleaning."

She shook her head, giving him an unsure smile. "No, I would rather make my own dresses. I like to sew. I find it soothing."

"Oh, well in that case, do you need more fabric?" he smiled. "You can go to the general store while I'm checking on Thad's clothes at the tailors. If sewing your own clothes is that important to you, I'm not going to take that away from you."

She gave him a bright smile, nodding her head. "That would be wonderful. Thank you."

"Good," he smiled back, walking her down the boardwalk a little ways, to cross the street in front of the sheriff's office.

Once he made sure Sadie was safely inside the general store, with Mrs. Harris watching over her, he turned to make his way back across the street, then toward the tailors.

He had only made it past the door to the café, when Michael Bayheart walked out and tipped his hat. "I see your brothers were right to set you up with that beautiful, young lady. You seem more like the old Tobias Townsend that I remember. The one from before you married Rachel Jones."

"What are you talking about, Bayheart?"

"Oh, come on, Tobias. You know me better than that," the man frowned. "Whatever happened to you calling me by my first name?"

"That was before you ruined the reputations of two innocent, young girls," Tobias snarled, crossing his arms over his chest.

"Innocent?" he scoffed. "I didn't ruin anyone's reputation. They done that themselves, when they made sure the whole town *heard* they had been with me."

"They were only trying to make you follow through."

"Follow through with what? I never touched either one of them."

Tobias snorted. "Are you trying to claim they

made it up?"

"Yep," he replied, propping himself against the side of the building. "Did it ever occur to you, before Miss Smith tried to force me into marriage, all the fathers in this town trusted me around their daughters, and most of the mothers were shoving those same daughters in my path on a daily basis. It's because I've never touched an innocent."

"Maybe you just never got caught before Miss Smith," Tobias shrugged, starting to doubt his own judgement.

Michael chuckled and shook his head. "I can see you are starting to see the truth, like your brothers."

"What about my brothers?" he asked with a scowl.

"They never believed all that mess."

"Yeah, I know. We had a few arguments about it," he said, furrowing his brow. "How did you know they set me up with Sadie?"

Michael chuckled. "Knowing how you believed I was such a defiler of innocent, young women, they asked me to be here to meet her, to make sure you didn't tell her, immediately, you were sending her back the next day. They figured you would do exactly what you did, to keep it from getting around town that you were putting her back on the stagecoach the next day." He chuckled again and shook his head.

Tobias managed his own chuckle over that. "I guess they know me about as well as one would expect. I'm also grateful they went through the trouble of such a convoluted scheme."

"Yeah, they were worried you were never going to get over what Rachel done. You do know, she was messed up, long before you married her?"

Tobias nodded. "That's what Cade keeps telling me. As a matter of fact, Jeremiah said the same thing a while back, as well."

Chapter 11
Thursday, May 20

Tobias left the general store turning toward the butcher shop. Before he made it ten feet, he was stopped on the boardwalk.

"Hello, Mr. Townsend," an older woman said, stepping into his path.

Tobias startled a bit, giving her a confused look. "Oh, good day, Ma'am," he said, moving to walk around her.

"Would you give me a moment of your time, please?" she asked, moving with him.

"I'm sorry, do I know you?" he asked, thinking he should be recalling her from childhood memories somehow.

"It's doubtful, Mr. Townsend. We've never actually spoken."

"Then what could you possibly need to speak with me about?" he asked, trying not to let his frustration show.

"Well, your first wife, that's what."

"My first wife? How did you know my first wife?" he asked, giving her a deep frown. "How do you even know I was married once before?" he asked after a second thought.

"I used to work for her father, as a maid. He hired me not too long after Rachel turned ten. I was there when his wife left him and went back east to live with her sister. I was dismissed about the same time you and Rachel got married."

"Okay, so what about Rachel? I can't see how there would be much to say at this point," he said, this time not bothering to try and cover his frustration.

"I'm guessing you knew before it was all over, that she never wanted to marry you."

"Yeah, I found that out when it was too late," he snapped, giving her a dark scowl.

"Did she ever tell you why she didn't want to marry you?"

"No, but obviously she found something wrong with me. I've come to the conclusion, she was just plain afraid of me."

"It wasn't so much you that was the problem."

"Really? You could have fooled me. She ran off, crying, on a horse that was way too much for her to control, and broke her neck."

"I'm doing a horrible job of explaining this."

"Well, I couldn't agree with you more there," he said on a deep sigh, shaking his head.

"She didn't want to marry *you*, because she was terrified of *all* men. Not just you."

"What?" he asked, the astonishment showing on his face.

"It wasn't just you."

"How could that be?"

"Well, it was her mother's fault," she sighed, shaking her head. "I really shouldn't speak ill of the dead."

"Her mother's dead?"

"After learning about what happened to her daughter, and why, she just gave up. The guilt ate away at her to the point she wouldn't eat. She could barely sleep. She just sat in the parlor all day, mourning. She was gone within a year."

"You said she felt guilty. What did she do?"

"Rachel's mother never really cared much for Mr. Jones, but she stayed with him until Rachel turned sixteen. She had finally had enough and decided she was going to go live with her sister. She wanted to take Rachel with her. Mr. Jones refused, saying Rachel would stay with him until he could marry her off to a wealthy husband. She got her revenge by making sure if he ever managed to marry her off, her husband would be sure to send her back weeks, possibly days later."

"How?"

"By making sure she feared the marriage bed. She told Rachel it was all very painful and disgusting, and that only the men ever enjoy it."

"Why would she do that to her own daughter?"

"Trying to stop him from selling their only child to the highest bidder. That's all Mr. Jones talked about for years. He wanted to find the wealthiest husband they could for Rachel. He wanted to share the wealth and power. He thought he'd found that in you."

"I still don't understand why she would do that to her own daughter."

"Elizabeth had been forced to marry for the same reasons. When her and Mr. Jones married, he was a lot wealthier. As a matter of fact, he was about the wealthiest from where he came from. It was old family money. He lost a lot of that wealth when he moved out here. None of his ventures paid off like he thought they would. He was a cold man, more focused on making money and gaining power than spending time with his wife and daughter. Rachel's mother wanted something different for her daughter. She wanted her to be able to marry for love."

"After what she did, that would never have happened either."

"I believe over time, Mrs. Jones would have relented, and explained things to Rachel. She would have admitted she lied. Unfortunately, Mr. Jones forced her to marry you, her pleas falling on deaf ears."

"I never knew. All I knew was, within twenty-four hours of our marrying, she was dead, and she had left a note that said she had never wanted to marry me. I always figured it was something with me that she didn't like."

"No."

"Why tell me this now?"

"At first, I blamed you, as well."

"I would have never married her, had I known."

"I know that now. I've learned more about you over the last four years. My point in telling you all of this is, you really need to give your young wife a chance. She came out here to marry. She's never tried to run from you." He just nodded his head, not sure what to say.

"Well, good day, Mr. Townsend," she said, finally turning to walk away. She was nowhere in sight when he finally realized he had never learned her name. She had, however, given him a lot to think about. And some hope.

Chapter 12
Thursday, June 10

Sadie was already up when Tobias climbed out of bed at five thirty, the sun just barely starting to rise. When he found her in the kitchen, already rolling out biscuit dough, he noticed she was extremely pale, and looked very tired.

"Sadie, how long have you been up?" he asked, the concern showing on his face.

She shrugged, not looking up at him. "Since about four thirty."

"Why so early?" he asked, crossing his arms over his chest. He gave her a pinched look, wondering if she had been throwing up again.

"No reason," she mumbled. "I was just having trouble sleeping."

"Having trouble sleeping?" he snorted, his irritation obvious. "You look like you haven't slept in a week."

She turned then, giving him a hurt look. "Do I really look that bad?"

He sighed, rubbing his temples. He had to keep reminding himself to be careful with what he said to her. She had been taking everything he said far more seriously than he intended it, of late. "You just look tired, is all. Why don't you go back and lay down? I can get Thad to finish the biscuits. And I'll help him get the rest of breakfast ready for all of us."

"No," she shook her head. "This is my responsibility. You all have enough to do without having to take over my work, as well." She was afraid if they had to start doing the cooking and cleaning again, it would be enough of a reason for him to send her back. If she were sick for the next nine months, being pregnant with his child might not be enough to persuade him to let her stay.

He walked over taking her hands in his. "Sadie, I know you've been throwing up. You need to rest."

She gasped, giving him an almost frightened look. "I'm alright, I promise."

He shook his head, wondering what it was she was afraid he was going to say. She couldn't help being sick. "Everyone gets sick at times. Please, go get some rest."

She took a relieved breath, then nodded. "Okay." She turned toward the door but stopped before going through. "I need some things from Harris'. Would it be possible to go today?"

He gave her a big smile, thinking maybe they were making some progress. This was the first time she had asked him for something without going through one of his brothers. "Sure. Once you have rested for a little bit, and we have all eaten. I'll get everyone started on what needs to be done today. Then, if you are feeling up to it, I'll take you into town, myself."

"Thank you," she smiled back, looking more like herself, already. "That sounds wonderful."

******

After resting for about an hour, Sadie got up feeling much better, and thinking she might actually be able to hold down something for a change. She walked out of the bedroom to find everyone had eaten, and the kitchen was clean, except for a covered plate of food sitting on the still warm stove.

No sooner than she had stepped in the room,

Wally had turned and sat the plate on the table and pulled a chair out for her. "Here you go, Sadie. Tobias wanted to make sure you ate something. He's been worried about your throwing up for the last few days."

"Oh, I'm alright. You don't have to wait on me," she smiled. "I'm sure you have better things to do."

"Tobias told me to make sure you were eating before I run out to tell him you are awake. You don't want me to get in trouble, do you?"

She smiled at the boy, shaking her head at his crafty words. She knew Tobias really wouldn't blame him for her not eating. "No, I guess not," she said, taking her seat so he could push her chair up to the table.

"Do you want some milk to drink? Or do you want coffee?" he asked, working really hard to keep a neutral expression. He had no memories of his mother being pregnant. He was still learning to walk when his little sister had been born. But the other night he overheard his brothers, Cade and Ezekiel, talking about how his mother had thrown up a lot when she was pregnant with Jolie. They were both thinking Sadie was pregnant, now. That was a conversation he was sure he wasn't supposed to have heard, but he was hoping they were right. *I would like, very much, not to be the youngest for a change.* Like his mother, his sister hadn't been around long enough for him to remember her much, either.

Besides, Cade and Ezekiel both said they thought Tobias might come around quicker once Sadie was pregnant. Another conversation he was sure he wasn't supposed to have heard.

"I think I better drink water with a little ginger in it," she grimaced. "It might help settle my stomach. Then maybe I can have some milk."

He gave her a big grin, darting over to get her a

glass of water.

"Wally, I need hot water, like for coffee," she said, stopping him before he pumped water into a glass. "It's the only way the ginger will get into the water."

He nodded his head, turning to get the kettle they used to heat water for coffee. Sadie always drank coffee with breakfast. If she wanted milk instead, he might just be getting that niece or nephew he was hoping for.

******

"Well, hello, Mrs. Townsend," Mrs. Harris greeted her as she stepped through the door to the general store. "How are you doing today?"

"Better than I did this morning," she smiled. "And please, call me Sadie. While I'm exceedingly happy to be married to Tobias, the missus sounds so formal. In such a small town, it seems so out of place."

"You think Sapphire Springs is a small town?" Mrs. Harris asked, giving her a big smile.

"I came from New York City. Maybe out here, this little town seems larger. I don't know. But where I come from, this is small. And most certainly, less formal. I love the differences. People out here are far friendlier."

Mrs. Harris chuckled. "Well, I'm glad you like all of us. You've definitely made a difference in that ornery Tobias. He's been a lot happier in the last few weeks."

Sadie blushed, but still managed a shy smile. "Well, I certainly hope so. I'm really happy here."

"So, what brings you in today, Sadie?" she asked with a wink.

"I need more fabric."

"You're making yourself another dress?"

"No," she shook her head, blushing some more. "I need fabric for baby clothes."

"Oh, I see," she smiled. "Does Tobias know yet?"

"No," she shook her head. "I wanted to wait a little longer. You know, to be sure everything is going to be okay. It's still early yet."

"Yes, I understand," she said, leading her over to the fabric. "We have some new fabric in that I think might meet your needs just fine."

By the time she and Mrs. Harris had looked through all the fabric and found what she wanted, Tobias had come back from his errands and was ready to go. Mrs. Harris was still wrapping up the last bit of fabric when he walked in the door. He noticed it, wondering what she was planning on doing with it, but didn't bother to ask her. She breathed a sigh of relief when she realized he wasn't going to say anything and gave him a big smile. "Hello, Tobias. I'll be ready when Mrs. Harris is through wrapping my purchases."

"That sounds fine. Do you feel like eating at the café, before we head back to the ranch?" he asked, picking up her already wrapped parcels.

"Yes, I'm feeling much better. That would be wonderful."

Chapter 13
Monday, June 14

Tobias frowned as he watched Sadie dash from the kitchen the same way she had for the last six days at this time. The first few days he had thought she was sick. By day four he had suspected something different entirely but had decided to give her a few more days to choose when to tell him. Now, on day seven, he was certain he was right. With a grim look on his chiseled features, he followed her down the hall to the water closet. He stood behind her, at the door, waiting for her retching to stop before he spoke.

"Sadie, do you have something to tell me?" he asked, uncertain how he felt right then. He wanted children, but after his mother died while having his sister, the thought of Sadie going through childbirth terrified him.

"No, I don't believe so," she mumbled, keeping her head down, not wanting to look him in the eyes.

"Are you sure about that?" he snarled. "I've seen a woman get sick like this before."

"I don't know what you mean," she said, taking a deep breath, trying to settle her stomach. "I'm fine."

"Why don't you want to tell me?" he snapped back, sounding almost hurt.

"There's nothing to tell," she said, still keeping her head down.

"Just how long have you known you were pregnant, Sadie?" Tobias asked, snarling at his wife as she hung her head over the commode.

She looked up at him, shaking her head. "I don't

know what you mean."

"Sure, you do. If you're far enough along for me to notice, there's no way you don't already know."

"I..."

"Don't try to lie to me again," he boomed, nearly rattling the walls of the little room. "How long have you known you were pregnant?"

"About three weeks," she answered, trying her hardest not to cry.

"What, does having my baby disgust you that much?" he snarled, wanting to pound his fist into the wall.

"No," she said, giving him a startled look. "How could you think something like that?"

"Then why are you crying?" he asked, throwing his hands wide.

"Because I was hoping you wouldn't notice until it was too late."

"Too late for what?" he asked, just sounding baffled.

"I was hoping by the time you realized I was pregnant, you would need the physical side of our relationship as much as I do, and you wouldn't be able to stop. It's really the only relationship I have with you. It's the only time I feel close to you, and now I'm about to lose that, as well."

She had stood, and now pushed passed him to leave, not realizing the stunned look she was leaving behind her.

******

"How did my wife know what I had said about getting her pregnant?" Tobias snarled at Ezekiel on his way through the barn door.

"I don't know what you're talking about."

"There's no way she could have heard from

anyone but you. I didn't tell anyone else. And we were out on the range when I said it. Not another soul for miles, but the horses."

"Maybe Gray Wind told her."

"You're not funny," he snarled.

"Would you, please, tell me exactly what your problem is?" Ezekiel snapped, finally getting his fill of his brother's snarly attitude.

"Sadie heard I was planning on getting her pregnant, then moving her back to her old bedroom," he grumbled, running his hand through his hair before putting his hat back on.

"And?"

"She's pregnant."

"That's what you wanted, isn't it?"

"Yeah, but she's known for three weeks, and I just figured it out today."

"So, what?" he shrugged. "It's not like you give her any reason to want to talk to you."

"She doesn't want me to move her back to her bedroom."

"Oh, no," Ezekiel said, slapping his hands to his face, feigning horror. "Whatever are you going to do? Your wife wants to sleep in the same bed with you, and she's not afraid of you touching her. How could your life be *so* horrible?"

"Shut up," he snarled, turning to storm back out of the barn. "Get started. I have something to take care of."

"Only if that something is your wife," he growled, slamming his fists on his hips.

Tobias didn't bother to turn back, he just kept going, heading back toward the house. His plainspoken brother had finally made him realize something. Sadie was neither afraid of him, nor disgusted by him. She wasn't running. At least not yet. But if he didn't set things right soon, she might.

He had reached the back door but stood there with his hand raised to the knob, uncertain how to proceed. After a few seconds, he shook himself deciding his course of action was obvious. The truth.

He opened the door slowly, not wanting to startle her, and found her standing at the sink with her back to him. "Sadie," he said in as gentle a voice as he could, knowing how hurtful he'd already been this morning.

"Yes?" she sniffled, refusing to turn around.

He walked up behind her and wrapped his hands around her upper arms, just so he could touch her. What he really wanted to do was, pull her into his chest and wrap his arms around her, but he didn't think she would let him, right now. "I need to talk to you, Sweetheart. Could you come and sit down, please?"

She nodded her head, unable to speak for fear she'd ask him if he was finally going to send her away. If he hadn't thought of that yet, she certainly didn't want to put the thought in his head, but she had no idea what else it could be. She had never seen him like this, except for in the bedroom. She turned to walk around him, still avoiding eye contact, and took a seat, laying her hands in her lap and lowering her gaze to the floor, not saying a word.

He sighed, pulling a chair out so he could sit facing her. All he wanted to do was take her in his arms and hold her close, but he knew he had a lot to make up for first. "First things first. If you have already moved your things, I want you to move them back to our room."

"What?" she gasped, finally looking up at him. "Now, you're resorting to cruel jokes. I know you don't want me now that I'm pregnant. The least you could do, is pretend I'm not even here, instead of tormenting me with the one thing you know I want."

Tobias slid off his chair to kneel before her. "It's not a joke, Sweetheart. I don't want you all the way down the hall from me. I need you close while you sleep, so I can keep you safe."

"You must have realized I am in love with you," she stammered, so emotionally distraught she couldn't even feel embarrassment at her own words. "This is..."

He had her on her feet and wrapped in his arms, before she could finish her thought. His mouth crashed down on her lips without mercy. He didn't know yet how he was going to make all this right, but he was determined now, that he would.

At first, she kissed him back, just grateful she had cleaned her teeth and rinsed her mouth out, after throwing up earlier. It didn't take long for reality to sit back in, though, and she pushed him away.

"Please, don't," she whispered. "This all hurts enough, already."

She whimpered when he tried to pull her back into his arms, and he let her go. For the moment.

"Sadie, I thought if I gave you children, you wouldn't leave me. I never dreamed he'd tell you what I said. I only said it because I didn't want anyone to know how I really feel."

"How do you really feel?" she asked, wrapping her arms around her waist and looking down at the floor.

"I love you."

She snorted, giving him a glare. "Right? It sure doesn't feel like you love me."

"I knew when I set eyes on you, I was in trouble. You drew me in immediately, but I was desperate not to love you," he sighed. "You asked me once about my first wife."

"Yes, but you never would tell me what happened to her."

"She died," he said, gently pushing her back down into her chair.

"How?"

"She fell from a horse she had no business trying to ride. She was running from me. We hadn't been married twenty-four hours yet. She left a note that said she had never wanted to marry me." He sighed. "That horse was every bit as big as Gray Wind, and she didn't have the good sense you did to ride him astride. That's probably why she couldn't stay mounted when he got startled. She had been riding all of her life."

She gasped, looking back up at him. "That is why you were so upset about my taking off on Gray Wind."

"Upset?" he questioned, shaking his head. "I was terrified I wasn't going to reach you in time."

She nodded her head, and swallowed, finally understanding something of her husband's emotions. "Why hadn't she wanted to marry you?"

"Her mother left her father and went back east to live with her sister. When her father wouldn't let her take Rachel with her, she made sure Rachel was absolutely terrified of the marriage bed."

"Oh, my," she gasped. "That's horrible."

He nodded his head and continued. "She begged her father not to force her to marry me, but her pleas fell on deaf ears."

"But that was hardly your fault," she said, furrowing her brows. "Or mine."

"I just very recently learned this part of the story. I always thought it was me she feared or hated. Not all men. I feared you would eventually feel the same way and want to leave me."

"Tobias, I love you. I do not fear you," she said, placing her hand on his cheek, and looking him in the eyes. "All I have ever feared since arriving here, is you sending me back east."

"I love you, Sadie. I will never do that."

Chapter 14
Tuesday, June 29

A knock sounded at the door, bringing Sadie's head up from where she was kneading bread dough. "Oh, bother. Thad, Wally, could one of you get the door, please? I've got bread dough all over my hands."

"Yeah," she heard hollered down the hall, accompanied by what sounded like a herd of stampeding cattle.

"I want to answer the door," Wally hollered just before she heard something crash to the floor.

"I'm older. I get to answer," Thaddeus replied, rather loudly.

"Boys!" she shouted in frustration. "Answer the door. Please, don't fight."

"Hello, ma'am. I'm Thaddeus." She sighed in relief. At least they were being polite to whoever was at the door. "I'm one of Tobias' younger brothers. This is Wally. He's our youngest brother."

"Well, it's nice to meet you both," she heard in greeting, coming from a very familiar voice. "Is Sadie home?"

"Yes, ma'am," they answered together. "She's in the kitchen. Right this way," Thaddeus continued.

Sadie had already turned to stare at the doorway to the front room by the time their visitor had made it there. "Momma?"

"Yes, Baby."

"How did you get here?" she asked with wonder.

"Your husband sent for me," she answered,

walking over to hug her daughter.

"He's not sending me back with you, is he?" She had finally started to relax, believing she had found her place. Now, she was starting to feel uncertain again. What if he had changed his mind, and decided he didn't love her after all? She didn't think she could survive that.

"No, no, no," Wally and Thad started in together. "Your momma's moving here with us," Thad said with a grin. "Tobias didn't want to leave her in New York all by herself, with no family, and with very uncertain living conditions."

"Since you are her only living family, and you are married to Tobias, that makes her our family," Wally continued. "Tobias decided she needed to be here with all of us."

"Your husband sent money and a train ticket for me about a month ago," her mother grinned, but shook her head. "He contacted Mrs. McBride and had her find me. I didn't realize you didn't know."

"Well, at first he didn't want her to know, because he didn't want her to get her hopes up. He didn't know how long it would take Mrs. McBride to find you, or how she would...," Thad paused in his explanation. "Well, how she would find you when she did," he finally finished with a small shrug.

"Then after he found you, he decided he wanted to surprise her," Wally shouted out of excitement. "We've been bursting at the seams, wanting to tell you," he added, turning a very bright smile in his sister-in-law's direction.

"Yeah, the little cabin we've all been working on is for your momma," Thad said, beaming with pride. "It's so she has a place of her own, but she'll always be close by, so we can all help take care of her, as well."

"Oh, my. This is so wonderful," Sadie said,

wiping the tears from her eyes. "I was so worried about you."

"You don't have to worry any more. I'm right here."

"I've missed you so much. And now you're going to be here when the baby comes."

"Baby? You're already pregnant?"

"Yes, Momma. I'm not showing yet, but it won't be long."

******

"So, how many brothers did you say there were?" Mrs. Johnson asked as she watched two large men walk in the kitchen, ask Sadie how long till supper, then walk on through.

Sadie smiled, understanding what her mother really wanted to know. "There are seven of them, including Tobias, who is the oldest. That was Zachariah and Josiah."

"My, but they are large," she said, putting a hand over her chest. "Is your husband that big?"

"Well, almost," she grinned. "He's certainly not small. Zachariah is one of the largest. Cade is actually bigger. However, we're not sure Zach is done growing. He is only twenty, and Cade is only a little bigger than him."

"Have I sent you to live with a bunch of giants?"

"Maybe," she chuckled. "But I assure you, they are all very *gentle* giants."

"Well, how big is your husband, anyway?" she asked, shaking her head.

"I'm about six feet three inches tall, according to my tailor," a deep voice sounded from the door to outback. In her surprise over the size of the brothers, she had missed it opening. "Thad and Wally told me you had arrived safely, Ma'am. I'm Tobias Townsend.

Your daughter's husband," he said, walking over to offer a hand in greeting.

When she started to rise, he shook his head. "No, don't get up. I'm sure you are tired after all your traveling."

"Well," she hesitated. "I was wanting to give you a hug for saving, first my daughter, and now myself. And when I got here, she told me she is already expecting my first grandchild. You are responsible for all my current happiness."

He smiled. "You can certainly have a hug, but if you hadn't sent your daughter out here, I wouldn't be as happy as I am, either." This time when she started to rise, he reached out, hugging her close. "These days, I have a lot of people to thank for my current happiness," he said, looking over at Thaddeus.

He let go of his mother-in-law and walked over to wrap his arms around his wife. "Hello, Beautiful. How are you feeling today?"

"I'm feeling wonderful. Since Thad has taken over cooking breakfast, and I can go at a slower pace in the morning, I'm not having as much trouble with the morning sickness."

"Good. I didn't like seeing you so pale and tired," he replied, kissing her on top of the head. "Do you need help with supper? I can come back and help you, once I've cleaned up a little bit."

Mrs. Johnson stepped forward, smiling at the couple. "You go on and get cleaned up for supper. I'll help her finish with the cooking."

"I couldn't ask that of you, Ma'am," Tobias started.

"Sure, you could. And call me mom, please. Not ma'am."

"Okay... Mom. But you've got to be tired after traveling from New York."

"Yes," she nodded. "But I'll survive a while

128

longer. Besides, it'll give me a few more minutes with Sadie, before we all sit down for supper."

"Well, if you're sure," he said, giving Sadie a quick kiss on the mouth, before leaving the kitchen.

"I see you two have already grown to love each other."

"Yes," Sadie agreed with a serene smile. "We had a rocky start, but we've come a long way."

"I can see that. He loves you very much. He looks at you the way your father used to look at me."

"Really?"

"Yes," her mother nodded. "I prayed, when I sent you out here, you would find love, but the most I really hoped for was that he would treat you well. I can see now, I have nothing to worry about."

Epilogue
Friday, December 29, 1876

Sadie stood at the counter, working on the bread dough, humming a Christmas song to herself when she heard the backdoor open. She turned and smiled as Tobias shook the snow off his cowboy hat and stomped it off his boots before coming on inside, trying to make sure most of the snow landed outside on the porch, before looking up to smile back at her. Once he was happy most of the snow was off, he came in, hanging his hat on a nail as he headed toward her.

"Hello, Beautiful. Something smells amazing."

"It's just beef stew. I figured as cold as it was out there, you all would need something hot and filling to warm up with."

"Stew sounds wonderful," he replied, taking his coat off to hang over the back of a chair.

"Tobias," she said, turning to fully face him, giving him a bright smile.

"What, Beautiful?" he asked, wrapping his arms around her and pulling her close.

She snuggled against his chest, wrapping her arms around his waist. "I have a surprise for you."

"What's that?" he asked, leaning down to kiss her on top of her head.

"You'll have to wait till supper time."

"Wait till supper time? Why?" he asked, sounding more curious than before.

"I want to tell everyone at once."

"Oh," he said, leaning in to kiss her on the mouth. It took him several seconds before he was ready to raise his head. "Is your mother coming over for supper?"

"Yes," she said, raising up on the tip of her toes to kiss him again. When their lips made contact this time, he groaned, picking her up to let her feet dangle several inches above the floor, and held her tight.

He heard someone clear their throat, and seriously thought about ignoring them. When they cleared their throat again, he sat her down on the floor, but didn't let go of her. He turned, his eyes on the man standing in the doorway, and glared. "What?"

"I just thought maybe you should wait till bedtime to continue," Cade grinned. "The rest of us would like to eat supper before it burns."

"Yes, I need to finish with the bread," she said, trying to hide her blush as she turned back to the counter.

"Sorry, Sadie. I didn't mean to embarrass you," Cade smiled. "How much longer till supper is ready?"

"I just have to get these rolls baked. It won't be much longer. Everyone should get cleaned up."

******

Sadie waited till everyone had taken their seats and they gave thanks for the meal set before them, before she brought up the *surprise* she had mentioned to Tobias earlier. Just as she was getting ready to speak, little Nathan threw his spoon and chanted, "Da, Da, Da, Da, Da."

Tobias looked over at his little son, and grinned. "Did he say dad?"

Sadie chuckled, and nodded her head. "He's been saying it all day. He looked so surprised when he said it the first time, it was just adorable. I wish you had been here. That's why I did not want to say anything before he said it where you could actually hear him. I wanted it to be a surprise."

Tobias looked back over at his little son, and smiled, running his hand over the little boy's soft hair. "Your first word, Little Man. Daddy's really proud of you."

"Yeah," Thaddeus chuckled. "Sadie's been trying to get him to say mom ever since."

"Is that the surprise you were talking about earlier?"

She shook her head, "No, there's something else I need to tell you. It just so happens, you get two surprises today."

He gave her a huge smile. "Well, what's the other surprise?"

"We're having another baby."

"Another baby?" he asked, sounding awed.

"Yes," she smiled, nodding her head, tears of happiness welling in her eyes when she noticed how happy her husband looked. She thought about how they had started out and glanced over at her brother-in-law. If it hadn't been for a certain stubborn teenage boy, she wouldn't be here. She wouldn't have everything she could have hoped for. Love and a wonderful family to share it with. For that one reason alone, Thaddeus would always be her favorite of the brothers. After Tobias, of course.

Tobias stood, pulling his wife from her chair. He pulled her close, hugging her tight. When he felt her giggle, he pulled back to look her in the eyes. "What?" he asked, smiling down at her.

"I guess getting married on Saint Patrick's Day proved to be lucky, after all."

"No, it's not luck, Sweetheart," he said with a shake of his head. "We're blessed." He kissed her on the forehead and pulled her against his chest once again. "I thank God your mom sent you out here to

me, not the luck of the Irish."
She nodded her head, squeezing him tight. "Yeah, me too."

If you enjoyed this book, please, be sure to leave a review on Amazon. Thank you!

Keep reading for a preview of the next book in the Townsends series. Thank you! Happy Reading!

Excerpt from Married In Vegas:

Prologue
Saturday, July 4, 2009

Jenny had her back to the door when she heard it open. It didn't matter. The second he stepped in the room, she knew without looking who it was. It was the most peculiar feeling. And she had never been able to get used to it. But ever since she was about twelve, when Mark walked in the room, if she had her back turned to him, she could feel it was him. His very presence would always send chills running up her spine. She still, to this day, didn't understand what those chills were trying to tell her. She had no idea they were both about to find out.

Her parents were having their annual fourth of July party, and everyone else was still outside eating. She had gotten tired of the heat from the summer sun, and decide she wanted to find something to watch. She was still looking for a movie when Mark stepped up behind her. He was close enough, she could feel his body heat coming off of him.

She shivered a little and did her best not to turn and run from the room. The nervous butterflies in the pit of her stomach was something new to go with the butterflies. "So, Mark, do you want to watch a movie with me?"

"Sure," he answered, humor in his voice. "But can you answer a question? I've wanted to ask for a while now."

She done her best not to give into the need to swallow nervously. "Okay. What do you want to know?"

"How do you always know it's me? You never have to turn and look. It's almost a little freaky how you do that."

"Thanks," she snorted. "A little freaky is putting it nicely." She could tell he was struggling not to laugh, and it made her more nervous. She ended up just saying the first thing that popped into her head. "I don't know. Maybe it's your size."

That just caused him to struggle harder not to laugh. He shook his head, a smile breaking out across his face despite his best efforts. "You've been doing this for a long time. The first time I noticed, I wasn't more than fourteen or fifteen. I know I was big for my age, but I've not always been this big. There's got to be more to it than that."

"I really don't know what it is. But I...," she shook her head unable to continue. "I don't think I should tell you." The more she thought about telling him, the more nervous she got.

"Oh, come on. It can't be that bad. Tell me." Her reluctance to tell him was making him more curious, causing him to take a step closer. It surprised him when he heard her breath catch, and he didn't understand why, but he had to fight the urge to step closer. He shook his head, his smile turning to a frown.

He managed to force himself to take a step back and give her more room. He was used to people being put off by his enormous size, but he had never noticed her reacting that way before. For some reason, that he didn't understand, that really bothered him.

"I'm sorry. I didn't realize my size bothered you," Mark said, sounding hurt.

Jenny could hear the pain in his voice, and she just turned around and stared at him for a few seconds, wondering if he had lost his mind. "It doesn't. Why would you think that?"

He gave her a strange look. He snorted and shook his head. "Jenny, you don't have to lie. I heard your reaction when I got too close."

"Oh, that had nothing to do with your size. That was my radar going into overdrive," she answered with humor in her voice that was aimed at herself.

"What do you mean by radar?" Mark asked, sounding puzzled.

At least he doesn't sound hurt anymore. "You're the only one it happens with," she said, turning her back to him. "But I can literally feel you when you walk in the room."

He just stood, staring at her back, wondering what that could mean. "You feel me, how?"

"You give me chills up and down my spine. Please, don't laugh at me. It's a physical reaction, and I can't help it." She pulled a movie out at random, without looking to see what it was, and walked over to the TV and DVD player. She just put the disc in the player before going to sit down on the black leather couch.

"I'm not going to laugh at you. I am a little mystified though." He stood there staring at her for almost a full minute, wondering what it could all mean.

She decided she was going to do her best to shake off the feelings caused by what she had just told him. She picked up the remote from the coffee table, and sat back, patting the seat beside her. "Come on, sit down."

Once the movie started, her expression turned sour. She wished she had been paying more attention. It turned out to be one of the sappiest romantic dramas that her parents owned. She hated sappy movies. She was an action junkie, through and through. Mark had finally moved over and sat down beside her, and now he was laughing at her.

"What?" she snapped, turning her sour expression on him.

"I know you. Were you not watching what you were doing? You hate these kinds of movies," Mark said, trying hard to stop his laughter.

"Fine. You pick something." Because of her already vulnerable emotions, she ended up snapping at him more harshly than was necessary. That just caused her expression to get even more sour, and now Mark was turning red with the effort it took him not to laugh.

"Okay, I will," he said, humor still in his eyes. Even if he did try to give her a reassuring smile before standing to his feet.

When he stood up, the hairs on his leg brushed her knee, and she gasped. It had been the softest feeling she had ever felt, but the jolt it sent through her was anything but soft. She sat there staring at his back while he removed the DVD from the player. She was still feeling dazed when he returned to the couch and sat down by her. It was all she could do not to jump away from him. She was still trying to process what had happened.

When the movie started, she was barely aware of

what was going on. All she was able to register was, it was an action movie. One of her favorites. There was a strong part of her that wanted to touch him again, just to see if it would happen again. She was trying really hard to think of some way to brush his leg with hers, and not look too obvious. She needed to know if it had been real or just her imagination.

If she had any idea what was going on in his head right then, she probably would have jumped up, and ran from the room immediately. It was crystal clear to him all of the sudden what her chills had been trying to tell her, and he realized he felt the same way. He was wondering how hard she would punch him if he leaned over and tried to kiss her.

The only reason he had done better with selecting a movie, was he was concentrating really hard on the task. Once he got sat back down, he wasn't able to pay any attention to the dialog at all, and the pictures seemed hazy to his mind. His concentration was focused totally on her, and the fact that she seemed to have gotten really jittery all of the sudden.

The harder she tried to think the more nervous she got. Finally, the nervous energy got to be so bad that she jumped up. She tripped over his foot and fell backwards, landing in his lap. It had defiantly been real she thought, as she lay there looking up at him, blinking from surprise. She closed her eyes, hoping she would be able to think more clearly. Instead, it made her more aware of his strong, solid body under her. When she opened her eyes, and looked up at him once again, she seen the same emotions she was feeling reflected back at her.

She heard him groan, and then the next thing she knew he had pulled her tight against him and ran his fingers through her hair. When his mouth came down on hers, she almost blacked out. It was all too much, but she couldn't stop herself from kissing him back. She brought her arms up around his neck and wove her fingers in his hair, holding on for dear life.

When his mouth moved away from hers, she felt a moment of panic until she felt his lips graze her neck. She wasn't anywhere close to ready to stop. Nothing she had ever felt had prepared her for how she was feeling right at that moment. He had kissed his way up her neck and was now working along her jaw. She was still trying to catch her breath when his mouth claimed hers again.

At first, when he started working his way back down her neck, she didn't realize they had shifted positions, and that she was now laying on the couch with him raised above her. All she could feel was his hot mouth as it moved down her neck once again. She had a vague thought that she needed to stop him when she felt him move lower, brushing his lips over the swell of her breast. But she was so overcome with the sensations he was creating, she couldn't form the words.

It took his warm hand coming up under her shirt, and brushing the sensitive skin of her belly, for her to realize they were getting way out of hand. She was going to have to stop him. "Mark," her voice broke over his name. "We have to stop. What are we doing?"

She heard him groan. And when he raised up, he took her with him. He had his face buried in the curve of her neck and had her pressed so tightly to him, she could barely breath. He seemed very reluctant to let her go.

When she tried to push away, he groaned again, and raised his head to look down at her. "Please, not yet. Just let me hold you." She could see the desire and passion still raging in his eyes. She understood how he was feeling. She was still feeling the same way herself. She brought her arms back up around his neck and buried her face in his chest. She really didn't want to let go of him either.

Chapter 1
Wednesday, July 3 (four years later)

"Jenny, Mark's already left for the day, and this is corporate on the phone." Jane managed to get Jenny's attention just before she walked out of the office door. She was the lead secretary, right under Jenny, in the office at Mark's hardware store. "Since you were still here, I haven't tried to call him yet."

Jenny turned around and looked at her with a look of confusion, and mouthed, "Corporate?"

"Yes," the older lady nodded. "Something about an emergency meeting," Jane said, shrugging her shoulders. "They wouldn't say anything else. I'm obviously not high enough up the food chain."

"Okay, I'll take it in the office," Jenny said on a sigh. She had a feeling she wasn't going to be happy about this.

Five minutes later she slammed the phone down with a disgusted look on her beautiful face, slouching down in her chair. "Boy, do they know how to screw up one of a girl's favorite holidays."

She pushed back from her desk, making her way across the room to stick her head out the door. "Jane, can you try to get Mark on the phone?" she asked, doing her best to remember this was neither the secretary's nor Mark's fault. "Try his home phone and cell both if you have to."

"Okay," Jane said, and turned back toward the phone.

A few minutes later, Jane buzzed Jenny in the office. "Jenny, he didn't answer either one. What do you want me to do?"

Jenny breathed out a heavy sigh. "Nothing. I'll go find him. There's not enough time. We have to be in Vegas tomorrow. Why they think having a meeting in Vegas is going to stop it from ruining everybody's fourth, I don't know. I think they're crazy. Either that, or they just want a few days in Vegas for themselves."

The older woman looked at her like she had lost her mind. "Vegas?"

"Yes, crazy isn't it?"

Jane shrugged her shoulders, giving her a friendly smile. "Well, I don't know about crazy, but what kind of emergency would require you to go to Vegas for a meeting?"

"I don't know. They didn't tell me, either," she grumped. "Apparently, we'll be told when we get there. I was just told at least we had Vegas to look forward to."

"Okay," the other lady whistled low. "That's the crazy part."

"Exactly," Jenny mumbled. "Make sure you're prepared for a day without me and the big boss tomorrow before you go home tonight. Call my cell if you need anything. You and the other two can run this place without too much fuss for the day. Hopefully there won't be any hiccups with the fourth of July sale tomorrow."

Jane chuckled, herding her out of the office. "We'll be fine. You and Mark we're only supposed to be on standby tomorrow, anyway. Go find the big guy and tell him the good news."

"Yeah, he's going to be so happy," Jenny snorted, waving over her head on her way out the door.

"You might be surprised," Jane whispered with a soft smile, watching the beautiful, young woman leave the office. *They just might come back married, if Mark has any say in the matter.*

Five minutes later she was crawling into her car, headed for his house. The thought of being alone with him there was making her more than a little nervous. They had a hard-enough time stopping when they knew they could be walked in on. There would be very little chance of that there, and she knew he would never pass up the opportunity to kiss her silly.

She had fretted about it so much, by the time she knocked on the door, she was all but shaking. She ended up knocking again before she heard him holler, "Just a minute. I'm coming."

The first thing out of her mouth when the door came open was, "It's work related. So, can we deal with that first, before you try and make... me... crazy." Before she had finished, her words had started to trail off. She had been so absorbed with her thoughts, it had taken a few seconds for her to realize he was standing there in a towel.

He just grinned at her, crossing his arms over his massive chest, and asked, "Why didn't you just call?"

"We tried, but there isn't time to try all night. You must have been in the shower," she mumbled to herself, blushing to her roots.

"Actually, I was in the tub, using the jets. Working with you all day tends to wind me up pretty tight. It's really hard not to grab you and kiss you when we're alone in the office," he said with a grin, watching her cheeks turn even redder. "I may have been in there longer than I realized."

"Do you often answer the door dressed in nothing but a towel?" she asked, getting even redder when her eyes strayed downward. She was finding it very hard to keep her eyes focused on his face.

"Nope. I looked out the window before I answered the door. I knew it was you," he said, looking at the clock. "What's this about? You mentioned something about not having enough time to call all night."

"You and I have to be in Vegas by, at the latest, one tomorrow," she answered, finally managing to shift back to business mode. "I figure any later than that and we're going to run the risk of being late for the meeting. It's at three."

"What meeting?"

"Corporate called after you left. I don't know what it's about. They said they'll let us know at the meeting."

"Yeah? Do they not realize it's the fourth of July?" Mark asked, his voice heavy with irritation.

"That's the reason they're having it in Vegas. They don't want to ruin everybody's fourth. I think they're crazy," Jenny said, irritation dripping from every word. "Do they think everyone in the known world likes to gamble? There are some people who have better things to do with their time, and money. Like spend time with their families. We're going to miss Thursday night family dinner," she grumbled, adding him, knowing he would have been there too, if not for this stupid meeting.

Mark just laughed. "I guess you're here to work out travel and overnight arrangements."

"Yeah. Do you think you could put some clothes on first? I need to be able to concentrate, and I'm going to be worried about you losing that towel the whole time if you don't," Jenny said, once again looking down, and flushing all over again. Then she said, a bit too honestly, causing herself to flush even more. "And thinking about taking it."

Mark reached down like he was going to pull it off, giving her a mischievous smile. "I'll give it to you."

"Mark, behave yourself, please. Go put some clothes on," Jenny said, somehow managing to get even redder than she already was. She was starting to feel like a giant, boiled lobster. She was certain she had to have heat radiating off of her skin.

Mark just laughed and headed back down the hall.